CURSE OF THE
DREAM WITCH

ALLAN STRATTON

ff

faber and faber

First published in this edition in 2013
by Faber and Faber Limited
Bloomsbury House,
74–77 Great Russell Street,
London WC1B 3DA

Typeset by Faber and Faber Ltd

Printed in the UK by CPI (UK) Ltd, Croydon CRO 4YY

A CIP record for this book
is available from the British Library

ISBN 978–0–571–28826–7

FSC
www.fsc.org
MIX
Paper from
responsible sources
FSC® C101712

2 4 6 8 10 9 7 5 3 1

For everyone who has nightmares

THE GREAT DREAD

It was the twelfth year of the Great Dread.

Once, the kingdom of Bellumen had been happy and safe. Feast days were celebrated late into the night in village squares, and children could fall asleep under the stars. No more. Now, youngsters who ventured outdoors after sunset were never seen again, and those who searched for firewood in the forest beyond the cornfields disappeared without a trace.

King Augustine, felled by a stroke, lay shrivelled in his sickbed. His wife, Queen Sophia, ruled in his stead. She claimed that strangers and wild beasts were snatching the children and had her troops patrol the streets and countryside.

It didn't matter. There was only one person the people blamed for the kingdom's misery: Princess Olivia. The Great Dread would only be lifted once the girl was gone.

*

The seeds of the Great Dread had been sewn on a cold, bitter midnight, thirteen years earlier, when King Augustine and Queen Sophia had slipped out of their castle in disguise. The king wore the woollen coat and cap of a peasant, and steered a small cart pulled by two billy goats. The queen lay at the bottom of the cart bundled in blankets and covered in straw. For years, the couple had prayed for a child without success. That night, they'd decided to seek the help of the Dream Witch who lived in the forest beyond the cornfields.

The countryside was fast asleep; the air still, except for the chattering of the king's teeth, the creak of the wooden cart wheels, and the clop-ping of the goats' hooves. All around, miles of cornstalks, shrouded in frost, shimmered in the moonlight.

They reached the bend where the road turned away from the forest. King Augustine helped his wife from the cart. 'Have we made a mistake? Should we go home?'

'Not if we want a child,' the queen said.

It was true. The enchantress was their last hope. Even the court wizard, Ephemia, hadn't been able to help. Older than old, she'd lost her spell books years ago; while she still recalled some magic words, she couldn't remember the order. It was too dangerous to experiment.

Queen Sophia nodded at the forest beyond the cornfield. 'Quickly. The witching hour will soon be past. Remember, whatever you do, don't stare at her nose.'

The couple held each other tight and edged forward. Dried stalks towered above them; husks rustled all around. A strange fog, smelling of rot, rose from the ground. Two red coals, like eyes, glowed through the mist.

The king and queen froze.

'What brings you here?' came a voice from the haze. 'What are your dreams?'

'Dream Witch . . .' King Augustine swallowed hard. 'We want a child.'

The sorceress chuckled. 'Your own or someone else's?' Her voice had a grating sound, like metal dragged across stone.

'Our own,' the queen said. 'Please.'

'Dreams can become nightmares.'

'Not our dream of a child.'

'You'd be surprised.'

The Dream Witch stepped forward; a great owl perched on her shoulder. She wore a cloak of woven bulrushes and a dirty, long-sleeved dress. Red-coal eyes burned on either side of her head. Under their glow, the king and queen saw her withered frame and long, curled fingernails. But what they mostly saw was her nose. Longer than an elephant's trunk, and twice as wrinkled, its base spanned the width of her forehead, descending between her eyes to her

waist, where it coiled around her body and looped itself into a belt.

She eyed them coldly. 'What are you staring at?'

'Nothing,' the king lied.

'Is it my nose?'

'No,' the queen insisted.

'It's rather big.'

'We hadn't noticed.'

'Why not?'

The king and queen hemmed and hawed and stared at their feet.

The Dream Witch enjoyed their discomfort. 'And you're sure of your dream?' she said at last. 'Your wish for a child?'

'Yes,' King Augustine replied, his voice as dry as a desert.

The witch scraped the kernels off a dried corn husk with her fingernails. She spat on them, muttered a few strange words, and gave them to the queen. 'Grind these into a porridge and eat it on the next full moon.'

'Thank you,' Queen Sophia's eyes filled with tears of gratitude. 'And what would you like for your reward? We'll give you anything for this kindness. We promise.'

The sorceress smiled. 'I shall let you know in good time.'

'Please, tell us now,' the king begged. 'We are a small kingdom without power or wealth. We'd hate to disappoint you.'

The Dream Witch waved a bony wrist. 'Fear not, your Majesty. I am a simple soul who lives in a humble cottage in the woods. My needs are few. A little keepsake – so small it will fit in my hand – is all I shall require. Now go.'

The king and queen did as they were told, and in due time the queen delivered a baby girl. They named her Olivia.

*

Olivia was a happy child. All day, she'd lie in her crib and gurgle. So much so that her parents feared she was simple.

The old court wizard, Ephemia, reassured them. 'All babies are like that,' she said. 'Wait till she's two.'

On the day of Olivia's christening, the royal family rode to the cathedral in an open carriage pulled by six white horses. The king's wig had rolls of plaited hair that spilled to his waist; his wife's was shaped like a swan. Baby Olivia was no less elegant in a white christening gown with purple piping and lace trim.

The ribbons in her parents' wigs caused the baby to point with delight. It was the first time her parents had seen her do anything besides burping. They prayed it was a sign of things to come.

At the cathedral, Olivia was nestled on a goose down pillow in a gilt pram. Everyone filed past to give her their gifts before the ceremony: Blankets from the weavers, bells from the blacksmiths, slippers from the shoemakers, and a very special present from Ephemia.

Although the good woman's spells could not be trusted, she still made the best *pysanka* in the kingdom. These hens' eggs, coated in colourful wax with bright squiggles, crosses, circles and lines, were said to provide protection against spirits. Yet only Ephemia's pysanka had the power to confound the Evil Eye.

The wizard placed a dozen of her talismans in a circle around Olivia's body. 'Precious child,' she said, 'may these protect you. Twelve *pysanka* for the twelve apostles, the twelve tribes, the twelve successors, and the twelve months of the year that roll us to infinity.'

She placed a finger in the baby's hand. Olivia gripped it tightly. 'See how fiercely she holds it?' Ephemia continued, the wrinkles in her smile more numerous than her years. 'She's a fighter. She'll go far.'

Suddenly, a bitter wind whipped black clouds across the sky. Thunder rolled – and the Dream Witch flew down on a giant meat cleaver, her hair as wild as a sea of snakes, her face as grim as a tombstone. Everyone dived for cover as the cleaver landed hard in the cathedral court-yard and sliced through the cobblestones before grinding to a stop near Olivia.

The king and queen stood between the sor-ceress and their child. Peasants cowered. Little ones hid their faces in their mothers' skirts.

A great owl landed on the witch's shoulder. 'I trust we're not too late?'

The bishop held up his silver staff. 'It is always too late for you, Dream Witch. Step not on hallowed ground.'

The sorceress ignored him. 'I'm here to claim my reward from the king and queen.'

'No! Depart, Impious One! Begone to your lair in the forest.'

The witch pinned him with a glance. 'You of all people should know my power, Bishop, you who came to me on the last new moon.' She waved her monstrous nose at the crowd. 'All of you, you come to the cornfield by my woods to make your dreams come true. You seek a spell to wither a neighbour's crops, or to speak to your dead, or to bring forth a child from a barren womb. Yet you who seek me out by night – you would deny me in the day?'

King Augustine stepped forward. 'No, we're true to our word. We promised you a keepsake, so small it would fit in your hand. What is it you want?'

The witch smiled. 'The heart of your little girl.'

The crowd gasped.

'Monster!' the queen exclaimed. 'Take anything else.'

'I *want* nothing else,' the witch said. 'The heart of a princess is all that I lack to cast the most powerful magic of all.'

'Seize her,' the king cried.

Guards leapt at the witch. She reared her trunk and trumpeted a mighty blast. The guards flew into the air. Another blast, and a powerful force bound the peasants to the ground and froze the king and queen like statues.

'Now to take my reward,' the sorceress said. She flashed her fingernails, sharp as steak knives. The crowd screamed. But when the witch drew near the baby, her hair scorched and her skin sizzled. 'Pysanka!' she screeched, and staggered backwards.

'Yes, Servant of Hell!' Ephemia declared. 'This precious babe is protected by my talismans.'

The Dream Witch peered down her trunk. 'Ah, if it isn't my old friend Ephemia,' she sneered. 'Are you still living? The centuries have not been kind. I remember when last we met; the night you dared enter my lair in search of spell books.'

'*My* spell books. Which you stole.'

'Which I *found* after you misplaced them. You were nothing without them then, and nothing without them now.'

'That's where you're wrong. For I have one remembered spell, and with it I send you to the Devil Himself!' Ephemia raised her wand. '*Prixus Amnibia Pentius Pendor!*' The wand splintered into a thousand pieces and Ephemia vanished in a puff of smoke.

The Dream Witch laughed. 'So much for meddlers.' She arranged her nose around her waist and turned to the crowd. 'Hear my curse: By the morning of the princess' thirteenth birthday, these twelve pysanka will be destroyed and I will have her heart. Until it beats in my hand, none of your children will be safe.

You shall live in terror, bound in a nightmare without joy, without happiness, without hope. I am the sum of your fears. Know me and despair.'

With that, she flew off on her cleaver. And the Great Dread fell upon the kingdom.

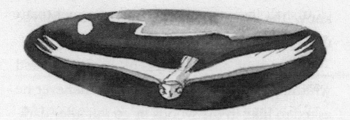

INTO THE WOODS

'Stop treating me like a child,' Milo demanded. 'Why can't I walk in the woods? In a month I'll be thirteen.'

His parents said nothing. His father sat in his rocking chair by the window of the little hut, whittling a bird carving from a piece of birch wood. His mother squatted on a stool peeling potatoes over a bucket. It was infuriating.

Milo struggled to control himself. 'I know children go missing,' he said calmly. 'But I'm older than them. And anyway, how do you know the Dream Witch steals them? Maybe they just run away.'

His mother and father kept on peeling and whittling. It was always like this. Whenever he asked to hike in the woods or go out after dark, they closed up like clams.

'Hello? Answer me.'

'Quit your nagging,' his father said without looking up.

Milo had had enough. 'Guess what?' he taunted. 'I'll bet those children *did* run away. Who can blame them? Working in the cornfields all day, being locked up all night. What kind of life is that? I should run away too.'

His father stopped whittling. His mother stopped peeling.

'Milo, please understand,' his mother said.

'No. I won't. All I understand is you don't care about me.'

'That's not true.'

'It is. Neither of you listen to a word I say. You don't know who I am or what I want. And you don't want to know, either. Well, you know what my dream is? To leave this place forever.'

He stormed to the door.

Milo's mother leapt to her feet. 'Where are you going?'

'To the cornfields. What does it look like?'

'Come back here,' his father barked.

'No. You don't own me. Not anymore.'

'Please, Milo,' his mother cried. 'Don't be foolish. We love you. We only want to keep you safe. If anything happened to you we'd die.'

'Hah!'

*

Milo had been born on the very same day as the Princess Olivia – almost thirteen years ago. But while she grew up in a castle, he was raised in a hovel. While she was destined to be a queen, he was destined to work in the cornfields. And while everyone in the kingdom knew her story, the only people aware he even existed were his parents and a few neighbours.

There were other differences, too. As a baby, Olivia was known for her gurgling; Milo for his kicking. He'd practically booted his way into the world, and immediately begun to explore. By the time he was a year old, his terrified parents had found him wedged in the woodpile, curled up with the piglets, and teetering on the lip of the well. They'd had to tie him by a rope to a fence post until he was old enough to pick corn.

A year ago, his father lost his right foot while chopping firewood. He'd carved himself a new one, but field work was impossible. Milo had dutifully tended the farm alone ever since. He fed the pigs and the chickens, fetched water from the well, planted and reaped the corn, and traded what he could at market. What with all the feeding and fetching, the sewing and reaping, the tending and trading, he never had any time for himself. Except at night, and then he was forced to stay inside because of his parents' fear of the Dream Witch.

Milo kicked a stone into the cornfield. He hated being angry. It made him feel stupid. Worse, it made him look childish, which is exactly what his parents said he was and what he wasn't. His parents loved him – he knew that – but all the same: *It's not fair*, he thought. *According to them, I'm only old enough to work. 'You can walk in the forest when you're older,' they say. Well when's older? What's older? I bet they'll be saying, 'Wait till you're older,' when I'm sixty.*

Milo closed his eyes and walked between two rows of corn. It was a trick he used to clear his mind when he was mad. The object was to take as many steps as he could without bumping into the stalks, turning left or right every fifty steps. His record was three hundred and twenty paces. Being scrawny helped – he easily fitted between the rows. Still, it was pretty amazing considering the fields ran over hills and some of the rows were uneven.

Today, skill and luck combined. Before Milo knew it, he'd counted three hundred and fifty steps – a record – and was still going strong. He was so focused on the game that memories of his quarrel had faded. Soon he was at five hundred steps. Then eight, nine – a thousand. A thousand steps and he hadn't once touched a corn stalk!

Milo burst with pride. He took three more steps and walked into a tree trunk.

What was a tree trunk doing in a cornfield?

Milo opened his eyes. Somehow he'd walked from the field into the forest. He'd dreamed of going into the forest but now that he was here he was petrified.

He whirled around. To his relief, the cornfield was only ten yards away. The sun was shining, the sky was clear, and butterflies fluttered on the corn tassels.

Milo laughed at his parents' fears. Here he was in the forest and the Dream Witch hadn't got him. Even if she appeared, he could easily run back to safety.

Milo decided to test his luck. 'Hello?' he whispered.

Silence.

'Dream Witch?' he called out with greater confidence.

More silence.

'YOO HOO, DREAM WITCH,' he sang, 'TELL ME MY DREAMS!'

A shiver of fear tickled his forehead. Was the evil one ready to leap from a foxhole or pounce from a rotten tree stump? He stopped and listened hard.

All was well. The sun still shone. The birds chirped freely.

Milo couldn't wait to tell his parents. He'd gone where they'd feared and what had happened? Nothing. They'd feel so foolish. From now on, he'd be free to come and go as he pleased.

Flush with excitement, Milo saw something glitter a few feet away on the mulch of leaves that carpeted the forest floor. A gold coin! Why, it was proof that someone had entered the woods before him.

Someone rich, Milo thought. *I wonder if the king and queen made up the stories of stolen children to keep us peasants out of the woods. That way, they could have it all for them and their friends.*

Milo picked up the coin and rubbed it till it gleamed as brightly as he imagined it might gleam in the king's own money pouch. *A coin like this will buy roast beef for every night of the year*, he beamed.

No sooner had Milo put the coin in his pocket than he saw another, twenty feet farther into the woods beside a puddle from the last big rain. He retrieved it and, to his amazement, saw a third coin far ahead on a rock.

Some poor noble has a hole in his money pouch. Well, finders keepers. Milo paused. *Maybe I should turn the coins in to the king instead. For my honesty, maybe he'll give me a place at court and my family won't ever have to worry about money again.*

Milo pictured a suite of rooms at the castle, his mother in silks and satins, his father with a new fitted foot from the royal carpenter, and himself knighted by the king. *Imagine, Sir Milo.*

It was a foolish fantasy; for *that* kind of reward he'd need a purse-full of coins.

Well why not? If the purse has a hole in it, there's bound to be more.

And there were. Milo found a fourth coin a few hundred feet ahead, near a cluster of berry bushes, and a fifth coin in a patch of brambles.

A great owl peered down at him from a hole in an old elm tree. It twisted its neck and hooted. Milo looked beneath its perch. To his delight, he saw a sixth coin lying on a cluster of mouse bones.

The owl ruffled its feathers and flew deeper into the forest. Milo hesitated. Six coins was a lot. Maybe it was time to go home. *But what if the owl is good luck? Ten coins. I'll stop when I have ten.*

He ran after the owl. But the owl's hoot was always a little farther than he could see, and he was slowed by thorn bushes, rocks and potholes. The hooting faded away into the distance. Milo decided to go home. The light was dim. The forest canopy hid the sun. Or could it be dusk?

Milo turned around. The cornfields were nowhere to be seen. In fact, there was nothing but trees – trees in every direction disappearing into darkness. A cold sweat trickled down his neck. *There's nothing to worry about*, he told himself. *I just have to go back the way I came.*

But which way was that?

Milo remembered he'd just passed three boulders on his left. Returning, they should be on his right. Only they weren't. The world had turned itself around and everything was opposite to what it should be. It was like walking into a mirror.

He heard a whistle of wind; felt a swirling around him in the brushwood. He froze. Maybe whatever it was would go away.

The sound stopped. Everything was still. Milo breathed a sigh of relief. He prepared to tiptoe away, when –

'Good evening.' The voice behind him was like metal grating over stone.

Milo's throat went dry. Deep down, he knew who it was, but he was afraid to face her. As long as he didn't see her, he could pretend she wasn't there.

'You have something of mine,' the witch said quietly.

Milo gulped. He fished the coins from his pockets, and held them out to her, head to the ground, eyes tightly shut. 'I'm sorry. I didn't know they were yours.'

'You didn't know they weren't.'

'I was going to turn them in.'

The witch chuckled. 'Because it was right? Or for a reward?'

Milo's legs began to tremble uncontrollably. He wanted to run, but he couldn't. Why did he have to be so scared? So stupid?

He felt the red-hot glow of the witch's eyes; the icy grip of her long, curled nails as she took his hand.

He pictured his mama and papa waiting anxiously at the door, calling his name as the sun went down, and running in panic to the neighbours. He imagined their howls filling the night.

Milo wanted to ask where the witch was taking him. He wanted to ask what she was going to do. What was the use? He'd have his dream: to leave home forever.

No matter where, no matter what, Milo knew he would never see his parents again.

AND THEN THERE WAS ONE

'Milo, where are you? Please Milo. Answer us. We love you. Where are you?' Deep in their bones, Milo's parents knew the truth. Their calls turned to sobs. 'Our son! The Dream Witch has our son!'

Neighbours joined their wails, and the neighbours of neighbours. Voice upon voice, the chorus of grief filled the night air, sweeping across the cornfields and throughout the town around the castle. Everyone knew someone who had lost a child and the disappearance of young Milo rekindled shared pain.

Princess Olivia gripped the ledge of her turret cell. Her pet mouse, Penelope, put a paw on her hand to comfort.

'This is my fault,' Olivia whispered. 'I deserve to be locked up. Not just to keep me from the Dream Witch, but for all the misery I've caused.'

Olivia's cell was fancier than most. Its single window had thick bars embedded in the stone sill; lead shutters that were locked at night; a heavy oak door that bolted shut; and sentries who barred the entrance to everyone except her parents. But it also had a wall of mirrored wardrobes filled with silk and satin dresses and a hundred pairs of shoes; bookcases lined with stories in hand-crafted leather bindings; and a large armoire where she kept the dolls of her early childhood.

And, of course, she had Penelope. The little mouse first appeared when the princess was in her crib and had stayed nearby ever since. Olivia would discover her hiding in a sock, or wake to find her curled up on her pillow. She was the closest thing to a friend that the girl had ever had.

'I wish things could be like they used to be, when everything felt safe,' Olivia said quietly.

Penelope nuzzled her hand.

*

Olivia had felt safe until she turned five. Before that, the Dream Witch had done nothing and the kingdom had pretended all was well. This amused the witch. She enjoyed seeing children believe the happy lie while their mothers and fathers lived with the Great Dread, wondering when or if she'd strike.

The witch chose Olivia's fifth birthday.

Olivia's parents had arranged a celebration in the town square. They sat with their daughter on a reviewing stand above the crowd, with the twelve pysanka in a festive bowl carved like a chicken.

A magician approached on stilts. He had a face like an apple, hair like straw, and the longest fingers Olivia had ever seen. The trickster waved a hand over the bowl and opened his mouth. One of the coloured eggs popped out. He plucked two more from thin air, another two from under his elbow, and a last from behind Olivia's ear.

'Put the pysanka back in the bowl,' the king demanded.

'I'm sorry,' the magician said. He returned the eggs and fled the square.

Back at the castle, Olivia learned the truth: Ephemia's talismans were all that kept her from the witch. The king and queen learned something, too: Six of the eggs were now made of wood. The magician had plucked fake eggs from the air. At the king's command, he'd put *these* in the bowl and had stolen the real ones.

The thief was caught by morning, but not before he'd broken the eggs for the Dream Witch in exchange for his dream of fame and fortune. He got his wish, though his fame was his crime and his fortune unhappy. King Augustine had a stroke and the first of many children went missing.

Olivia was kept in the castle with the six re-maining pysanka locked in a metal box. One day, a servant boy knocked it over and all but one of the eggs cracked. The king had a second stroke and all children were banned from Olivia's presence.

The last pysanka was placed inside a silver pendant lined with velvet to protect it from falls. A maid was caught trying to steal it by sneaking it out of Olivia's room under some laundry. Her nephew had been kidnapped by the Dream Witch who'd demanded she bring her the pysanka, or the boy would be ground up for pies.

Olivia's father suffered his worst seizure yet and was no longer able to move or speak, except by tapping his left thumb. Her mother wrapped the last egg in a ball of wool and hid it in the turret cell at the bottom of a box of ribbons at the back of a shelf.

'Forgive me,' she said to Olivia, 'but I must lock you here to keep you safe. Don't worry. I'll keep you company at all your meals, and servants will carry your father up to join us on Sundays.'

Even so, it meant Olivia, now twelve, had

spent most of her time alone with Penelope and her books. Just like today.

Penelope curled up in Olivia's palm. The pair watched the parade of torches heading to the forest. This always happened when a child went missing: The family and family friends of the child tried to rescue their young. But the moment their torches entered the witch's forest, their homes burned instead.

Olivia shook her head in sorrow. 'It's useless. Why do they try?'

There are some things you just do.

Olivia looked at her friend in shock. Had Penelope spoken? The mouse blinked twice and fussed with her whiskers. *No, impossible*, Olivia thought and rubbed the creature's ear.

'The world should live without fear,' she said. 'One day it will. I'll face the Dream Witch. One way or another the kingdom's nightmare will be over.'

AN UNWELCOME SURPRISE

The next afternoon, Olivia sat at the marble table in her room, eating jam tarts with her parents. Penelope perched on the princess' shoulder, nibbling crumbs from her hand.

King Augustine had been bathed, shaved, and dressed in his military uniform. He was held upright by sturdy clips that secured his epaulettes to the back of his portable throne. Olivia tried not to notice how his cheeks and chest had shrunk, or how his mouth hung sideways.

Queen Sophia sat beside her husband, feeding him and stroking his right hand. She stroked it all the time, as if her touch might bring it back to life. The sight was hard for Olivia to bear. It drew attention to the hand's stillness, its shrunken muscles, and the thick blue veins that stood out against its pallid skin.

At least her father could still communicate. One tap of his left thumb meant 'yes'; two, 'no'. And, as always, his feelings flew through his eyes as quick as songbirds. The sparkle in those eyes helped Olivia to remember his laugh and the tender 'good nights' when he'd tucked her into bed and looked at her just so.

'I wish you'd keep that thing in a cage,' the queen said with a nod at Penelope. 'Especially when we're eating.'

The princess glanced at Penelope. 'You won't steal Mother's tart, will you?' Penelope sat on her haunches and scratched her ear with a back paw. 'You see? That means: "Of course not, I'm a lady."'

'Hah,' her mother said, 'I think it means, "I've got fleas."'

Penelope sniffed and turned her back on the queen. Queen Sophia smiled despite herself.

Olivia beamed. Her mother's tolerance of Penelope, especially around food, was a true sign of love.

The queen set aside her plate and tapped her lips with her napkin. 'About tomorrow . . . the day before your thirteenth birthday . . . we have a big surprise.'

Olivia put down the end of her tart. Her mother had never mentioned her thirteenth birthday, as if ignoring it could make the witch's curse disappear. Why mention it now?

'You're going to have a visitor,' her mother continued. 'Prince Leo of Pretonia. He's about your age; a year or two older, maybe. You'll like him. His father is sending him with his uncle, the Duke of Fettwurst, and a retinue of several hundred.'

'Are they coming to reinforce the castle?'

Her mother's smile teetered, like a toddler on skates. 'Don't be silly.'

'I'm not. The Dream Witch said my talismans would all be gone by my thirteenth birthday. And when they are, she'll have my heart.'

King Augustine's eyes darted between his wife and daughter.

Queen Sophia stiffened. 'We won't have that kind of talk.'

'I'm only saying what everyone knows,' Olivia said. 'It's why I'm locked up. Honestly, Mother, do you think pretending everything's fine will protect me? I'm not a child. Even if I were, I'm not stupid.'

The queen gripped the king's hand as if it were a cane. 'Prince Leo and his uncle are coming as guests to your celebration. The following day, they'll take you back to Pretonia as a birthday present. A holiday. You'll have fresh air. A chance to see the world beyond this turret.'

Olivia fiddled with her spoon. There was something her mother wasn't telling her. What was it? She was afraid to ask, but the not knowing made the secret worse.

'Your pysanka will come too, of course,' the queen continued. 'Each of Prince Leo's soldiers will have a copy, each in its own identical silver casing. Several hundred decoys will ensure your safety, so please don't worry.'

'I won't. I always feel safe when you're around.'

'We won't be coming,' her mother said gently. 'Your father's not well enough to travel and I'm needed here to rule the kingdom.'

'But you have to come.'

'Olivia. Please. A trip on your own. It's so grown up.'

'No!'

'I'm sorry,' the queen said. 'It's been de-cided.'

'Then un-decide it.'

'After Prince Leo and his uncle have travelled all this way?'

Olivia banged her spoon on the table. 'There's something you're not telling me. What?'

'I'm sure I don't know.'

'You do! Tell me!' But in her heart she already knew. 'Oh Mother! You plan to marry me to that prince, don't you? You're sending me far away where I'll never see you again.'

'That's not true.'

'Why do you always pretend things aren't the way they are?' Olivia roared. 'Why do you lie to me? To shut me up? To make me feel better? Well I don't feel better and I won't shut up.'

'Please understand,' the queen pleaded.

'No!'

'There's a wizard in the Pretonian court far stronger than any in our kingdom. You'll be out of danger. Free as the wind.'

'I don't care. I want to be with you and Father. Please! Just the three of us, forever and ever.'

'It's not possible, my love. Why, even if you stay at home, your father and I won't always be around.'

'But you have to be. I need you.'

Her mother's voice broke. 'One day, Olivia, you'll be all grown up and your father and I will be but a memory.'

'No!'

'It's the way of the world. In the meantime – now – there are others who can take better care of you than we can. We're giving you the chance of a new life. A real life.'

'A real life? Trapped in marriage to a stranger?'

'You don't have to marry. We promise,' the queen insisted. 'In Pretonia, you can see if you like Prince Leo. If you do, you have our blessing. If not, you can remain as a guest.'

Olivia didn't know where to turn or what to think. She dropped to her knees beside her father, took his left hand, kissed the palm, and pressed it to her cheek. 'Father, is this what you want, too?'

Her father gazed at her with sorrow. He tapped her cheek gently, once.

Olivia shuddered. 'But do you promise I won't have to marry?'

One firm tap.

'Good. And I can come home again?'

Her father paused. Tears welled in his eyes.

At that moment, Penelope hopped from Olivia's shoulder onto the king's hand. She scampered up his arm and nuzzled her nose into his ear. For a second, he was startled. Then his eyes cleared. His mouth twitched.

'Olivia,' the queen squirmed. 'Your mouse. It's tickling him.'

'No,' Olivia said in awe. 'Father's smiling. I think Penelope's told him something.'

'What an imagination.' Her mother swooshed the air and Penelope scurried back to Olivia's shoulder.

'Whisper in *my* ear. Please,' Olivia begged her friend.

But Penelope just blinked as if to say: *Are you crazy? I'm just a little grey field mouse. Aren't I?*

IN THE WITCH'S LAIR

Milo roused. What time was it? The room was so dark he couldn't tell. All he knew was that he'd had the most terrible nightmare:

He'd been in the forest and the Dream Witch had caught him and brought him to her cottage. Milo shuddered at the thought of it. The outside door was a mouth. Not something that looked like a mouth, but a *real* mouth. And inside was an earthen stairway that swallowed him into her underground lair. The witch flew him through a fog filled with the howls of evil things, over vast dreamscapes of jungles and castles and lava pits, then into a terrible darkness.

Like this darkness.

Milo rolled onto his side. Strange. He should be feeling his straw mat, the one in his corner near the stove where he must have fallen asleep. Instead, he touched a floor of cold metal that seemed to be cut into sharp triangular slats. Where the slats met, he felt a thick iron pole. He ran his hands up it. Just over his head the pole went through a ceiling.

Milo's heart beat fast. Where was he? What was the last thing he could remember from yesterday? He'd been in the forest. And it was dark. And he'd turned to go home. And . . . and then what?

He tried to remember a return, his parents scolding him, eating supper. He couldn't. All that came next was his dream. His throat went dry. *Please let it not be true. Please let me still be asleep.*

Milo became aware of a curious sound: Whimpers from somewhere beyond, from the left and the right, above and below. He took two steps across the metal slats and hit a wall of glass. He groped his way to the right and found himself moving in a circle. He was in a glass cage. A *bottle*. He tried to smash it with his fists but the glass was too thick.

'Let me out! Let me out!'

At the sound of his cry, the murmuring stopped.

A girl's whisper echoed out of the silence: 'You're awake.'

Milo pressed his face against the glass and squinted. 'Who are you? Where am I?'

'Don't ask,' said a boy. 'Shh.'

In the distance, Milo heard the creak of a great iron door on rusty hinges. A dull light, thick as plum jelly, filtered through the room. Milo gasped. He was in an enormous cave. Facing him, were shelves of children, rising up into the shadows, each child in a glass jar like his own.

'Asleep, my poppets?' a voice growled in the entranceway.

Milo froze. It was the voice from his nightmare. The voice of the Dream Witch.

'Don't try and fool me. I know your secrets,'

the Dream Witch purred. 'Some say the walls have ears. Well, mine really *do*.'

The sorceress advanced, growing taller with each step. By the time she reached them, she towered to the top of the cavern. 'I've come for some spice for my spell of the day.'

The children shook with terror; their jars rattled on the wooden shelves.

The Dream Witch pulled a hankie the size of a bedspread from her sleeve and smoothed it on the ground with fingernails as long as corn-stalks. Then she unfurled her nose from around her waist. It rose in the air and tapped the jars on the highest shelf. 'Hmm. A pinch of this? A pinch of that?' The trunk curled around a jar and brought it in front of the witch's eyes. 'Hello, my sweet.'

'Not me. Please,' came the little voice inside.

The sorceress took the jar in her hands and held it over her handkerchief. 'Don't worry, I won't take much.' She cranked the top as if it were a pepper mill. Tiny shavings fell out onto the cloth below.

'Ow. Ow.'

'Hush now,' the Dream Witch laughed. 'Why do you need toenails? Why toes? It's not as if you're going anywhere.'

She put the bottle back on its shelf, tucked the handkerchief up her sleeve, and leaned towards Milo. Her right eye filled the glass wall in front of him. He felt the heat of its red-coal gaze. 'Last in, first out,' she smiled.

The Dream Witch lifted his jar from the shelf. In horror, Milo realised that the metal slats he was standing on were grinder blades. He clutched the pole at the centre of his jar and hiked up his feet.

'It wants to live, does it?' The Dream Witch shook the container and he fell back to the bottom.

Milo froze as the witch sailed him down a stairway of coal into her private spell chamber, a cavernous room that seemed to rise into an inky night. All around was a jungle of clutter. Leather spell books lay scattered in heaps. Hobnailed boots, cloaks, and conical hats were tossed among baskets of herbs, bundles of chicken's feet, and boxes of beaks and rotting animal parts. Goat heads and monkey skulls peered from crevasses in the rock wall. Eyeballs stared out of pickle jars. The walls were worse, lined with terrifying murals of the witch's dreamscapes. Their monsters within prowled the canvases as if eager to leap into the room.

But worst of all was the larger-than-life mosaic of the witch on the far wall. It twitched and wriggled as if alive. In fact, Milo realised, it *was* alive. Snakes and worms, frogs and toads, newts and salamanders, and beetles and bugs of every description had been painted and pinned on a massive board of petrified oak. The creatures struggled to escape. Beetle-warts spun on their pins; moths and butterflies fluttered helplessly.

The Dream Witch rolled her eyes at the mess. 'Order,' she commanded.

The hobnailed boots instantly lined up in formation, and clicked their heels; the dirty clothes suspended themselves, shoulders hunched, chests in; the goat heads lurched upright, and the musty spell books flew into the air like falcons. The flapping covers choked the air with soot and dust as the books rearranged themselves into stacks around the witch's spell table.

Milo gasped at the table. Carved from a massive oak stump, it was as big as the village square and lit by a candle that flared like a bonfire. The Dream Witch set Milo's grinder down between a vat of blood disguised as an inkwell and a sheaf of parchments stitched together from the wings of dried bats. Then she unscrewed his lid and spilled him onto the table. Gusts of wind swirled about the chamber. Milo shrank against the inkwell as the witch's owl descended to her shoulder.

'Look, Doomsday,' the witch cooed to the owl. 'We have a new visitor.'

'Am I to be its mouse?' Milo trembled.

'Not yet,' the sorceress grinned.

Milo shuddered. 'What do you want from me?'

The Dream Witch plucked a tail feather for a quill. 'A little help.'

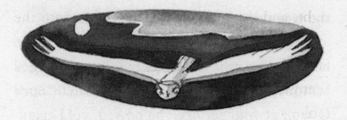

THE DREAM VISITOR

That night it took Olivia forever to fall asleep. At times, she thought she hadn't slept at all. But she must have, because she imagined it was the middle of the afternoon and Prince Leo and his uncle had come to visit her in her cell. This might have made sense, except Prince Leo had the head of a toad.

'You'll love Pretonia,' Leo said. 'We have so many bugs.' His tongue flew across the room and snatched a fly from a window bar.

Olivia sat bolt upright in bed. The lamp in the corner cast enough light that she could see she was alone. It was a dream. Good.

She tossed and turned some more. Suddenly, her old Christmas nutcracker leapt out of her armoire, only he was the size of a man. 'Count Ostroff at your service,' he bowed, gold epaulettes flashing in the candlelight. 'Might I have this dance?'

Olivia squeaked. Somehow she had white whiskers, grey fur, and a tail.

She screamed and found herself alone at her wall of closets. She glanced at the mirrored doors. To her relief, she looked the same as always. But how had she got there? Was she still in her dream? Had she been sleepwalking? Heart pounding, she slid back under her duvet. These dreams were far too real and far too scary. She decided not to fall asleep again.

But she must have drifted off, because the next thing she knew a gust of wind blew open the lead shutters over her window bars. These were always locked at night, but not now.

A great owl had landed on the windowsill with a scrap of parchment in its talons.

'Go away, Doomsday! Shoo!' Penelope scolded, clawing at the paper.

The owl tried to snatch the mouse with its beak, but the creature darted in and out between the bars.

'Penelope!' Olivia plucked her friend from danger.

The owl hooted, dropped the parchment on the sill and flew off. The parchment blew in through the bars.

'Rip it up! Throw it away,' Penelope cried.

'Penelope. You're talking!'

'Of course I'm talking. Why shouldn't I talk? This is a dream, isn't it?'

'Yes,' Olivia said. 'My third of the night. And I plan to wake up.'

'Fine. But before you do, get rid of that parchment.'

'If it's part of a dream, why should I care?'

'Just do it!' Penelope squeaked, running in circles.

To calm her down, Olivia put her in the drawer of her night table. Then she picked up the scrap of parchment. It was unlike any she'd ever seen, dark and delicate with a web of little veins. Why, it had been stitched together from bat wings.

There was a drawing on it: A thatched cottage surrounded by a picket fence. Large windows framed its rounded door; a flowering vine grew on its walls; smoke curled up from its chimney. When Olivia stared at the smoke, it drifted off the parchment; when she blinked, she could swear the cottage moved.

Well why not? Olivia thought. *It's a dream, after all.*

She tossed the parchment into her armoire, where she imagined it would disappear to wherever dream things disappeared to. Then she closed her eyes.

'At the count of three I will wake up,' she announced. 'One. Two. Three.'

This trick usually worked, but not tonight. When Olivia opened her eyes, she was still beside the armoire. And there was a knocking coming from inside it.

'Count Ostroff, go away,' Olivia exclaimed. 'I didn't want to dance with you in my other dream, and I don't want to dance with you now.'

'Who's Count Ostroff?' The voice in the armoire sounded like a boy.

'Don't you toys know each other?' Olivia demanded. 'He's the Christmas nutcracker. Which one are you? The china shepherd boy or the chimney sweep made of pipe cleaners? Whichever, you don't frighten me. I'm asleep and you're just a bit of food that went down the wrong way at supper.'

'I'm not trying to frighten you,' the voice said. 'Can I come in?'

'Do what you want. As soon as I'm awake you'll be gone anyway.'

The door to the armoire opened and a boy came out. He was about Olivia's age, tanned and lean, and possibly quite handsome. It was hard to tell because of the filth. His hair was so caked with dirt it could grow tomatoes.

'Am I where I think I am?' the boy asked.

'That depends,' Olivia said. 'Where do you think you are?'

'In the castle. Are you the princess?'

'Why?'

'I've come to rescue you.'

'Really?' The boy seemed very nice and Olivia thought it would be wonderful to dream about being outside. Maybe she wouldn't wake up so soon after all. 'Why do you want to rescue me?'

The boy looked confused. 'Because that's what I'm here for.' He saw the window and ran to it. 'My home,' he pointed through the bars. 'It's somewhere out there by that cornfield near the forest. Come with me? Please? Papa could whittle you a duck, or Mama could knit you a scarf, or whatever you like.' Out of nowhere, he began to tremble. 'Mama and Papa – they don't know where I am. Or how I am. Or even *if* I am.'

'Are you all right?' Olivia asked.

'Yes. No. It's all my fault.'

What an odd thing for a dream boy to say, Olivia thought. She began to wonder if maybe he was real. But that was impossible. Her armoire was made of solid oak; there was no way he could have sneaked inside. 'How did you get here?'

'I can't say.'

'Can't or won't?'

There was a pounding on the door. 'Olivia?' It was the queen. 'Are you all right?'

'Yes, Mother. I'm just having a nightmare.'

'You're what? I'm coming in.'

'I can't be found,' the boy gasped. 'We've got to go.'

'We?'

'Yes. You're my only hope. Come with me or I'm done for. So are my parents.'

'Don't be silly. Mother won't hurt you.'

'I don't mean her.' He raced to the armoire. 'Come now.'

'No.' Olivia twirled her hands. 'This is too fast. Ask me tomorrow.'

'Tomorrow?'

'Yes, if we're in the same dream. I promise.'

The key turned in the lock.

'Quick, before you go,' Olivia exclaimed, 'what's your name?'

'Milo.'

The armoire door snapped shut as Queen Sophia burst into the room followed by four soldiers with raised swords and lanterns. 'Olivia?' Her mother swooped her into her arms.

The princess wrestled herself free. 'I'm fine, Mother,' she whispered fiercely. 'Don't treat me like a baby. Not in front of people.'

'The guards heard voices.'

'I must have been talking in my sleep.'

'Those shutters. What are they doing open?' The queen waved her hand at the window; a soldier locked them.

'I don't know, I've been sleeping. Nothing's happened. I had a few nightmares, that's all.'

'The Dream Witch came to you in your sleep?' the queen gasped in alarm. 'I might have known she'd find a way.'

'Mother, no, calm down. They were silly nightmares. Prince Leo was a toad, I was a mouse, and a boy popped out of my armoire to rescue me.'

'A boy? Your armoire?'

'He ran back inside when you woke me up.'

The queen threw open the armoire door. There was no one there. She tore at the racks of dolls and toys until she could see the bare oak walls.

'I told you, it was a dream!'

The queen sighed in relief. Olivia suddenly realised she was in her nightie and wrapped her arms around her chest. 'Mother. Those men.'

The queen shooed the soldiers away and Olivia got back into bed.

'May I sit with you?' her mother asked quietly.

Olivia nodded. She propped herself up against a pillow.

Her mother sat beside her and smoothed a ringlet from her forehead. 'Forgive me. I should be giving you strength, not scaring you out of your wits.'

'It's all right.'

The queen shook her head. 'No. These last few weeks . . . as the curse gets closer. . .' She looked away.

Olivia took her hand. 'I know.'

Her mother hugged her tight. But instead of holding her to her chest, as she'd always done, she rested her head on Olivia's shoulder.

Olivia knew she should do something, but she wasn't sure what. Slowly, she began to stroke her mother's hair. Before either of them knew it, they were asleep and it was morning.

BACK IN THE BOTTLE

The Dream Witch reared her nose and loosed a blast that shook her underground study. Her spell books cowered. The creatures on her living portrait froze on their pins. 'I offered you freedom for a favour, but you failed.'

Milo pressed his hands against the glass walls of his grinder. 'I did my best.'

'If that was your best, what use are you? Farewell.' The witch gave the top of the grinder a twist. The floor of metal blades spun beneath Milo's feet.

'No wait,' Milo yelped. 'I can do better.'

'That's my boy,' the witch cooed. 'If bringing the whole girl is too hard, just bring me her heart.'

Milo shuddered. Before his visit, the witch had made his task sound noble. Olivia wasn't human, she'd said, she was a curse: The cause of the Great Dread, the kingdom's misery, the missing children, their weeping parents. But Milo couldn't think that now, not now that he'd met her. The princess was a child like him, only nicer. *She wouldn't hurt her parents like I have*, he thought. *She wouldn't say things to break their hearts*.

Milo filled with shame. 'Please, let me get you the heart of a sheep instead.'

'For that I could go to the market,' the Dream Witch laughed. 'Or save the bother and pluck *your* heart.'

'Why don't you then?' Milo blurted. 'You've taken everything else I care about.'

The Dream Witch arched an eyebrow. 'You're a little too young to play the hero.' She scraped her fingernails down his grinder. The glass shrieked. Milo covered his ears.

The witch held his jar in front of her face; Milo sweated from the heat of her red coal eyes. 'If you can't stand the squeal of glass,' she purred, 'how can you stand the howls of your mama and papa as they die of grief? Bring me the princess, or it shall be so.'

'If I do what you want,' Milo whispered, 'who says you'll keep your promise? Who says I'll be free and my parents safe?'

'How dare you question my honour? You deserve a good shaking. That'll knock the insolence out of you.'

The witch gripped the grinder with her nose and shook it for all it was worth. Milo bounced from top to bottom and back again.

What should I do? he wondered in horror. *What?*

THE TOAD PRINCE

Prince Leo and his uncle, the Duke of Fettwurst, arrived at Olivia's castle at noon with two hundred of their most battle-hardened soldiers. They were greeted at the gate by the queen and introduced to the king, who'd been transported from his sickbed in a ceremonial litter.

Olivia watched the proceedings through a spyglass from her turret window. She took particular interest in Prince Leo, the fifteen-year-old who was apparently to be her new friend, and in his uncle, the Duke of Fettwurst, who was to escort her to Pretonia.

Leo wasn't exactly a toad. All the same, he was slimy with spots. Sweat dripped from his pasty cheeks, while his pimples glistened like ripe cherries. The duke was worse; a walking sausage of cysts, his hands and neck matted with hair as thick as sauerkraut.

Olivia hoped they'd bathe before lunch. They didn't.

While their soldiers set up tents in the castle courtyard and servants brought their luggage to their guest quarters, Leo, his uncle, and a rumble of bodyguards were escorted directly to her cell. When they entered, the room filled with the stink of old cheese.

The queen slipped a perfumed handkerchief into Olivia's hand. 'Our guests couldn't wait to meet you,' she said. 'May I introduce Prince Leo and his uncle, the Duke of Fettwurst. Your Royal Excellencies, my daughter, the Princess Olivia.'

The duke nodded to Olivia. 'Your Royal Highness.'

'Your Excellency.'

Leo smirked at her and mumbled something.

'Thank you?' Olivia replied.

The duke beamed at the queen. 'Shall we leave the children to get to know each other?'

'Alone?'

'Of course not. With our royal chaperone, Lady Gretchen,' the duke winked. 'Our Leo's been known to turn a girl's head.'

'I'm not surprised,' the queen said diplomatically.

Leo pursed his lips. 'Father's placed my picture in castles all over Pretonia. Girls like it.'

Olivia pretended to sneeze, gasping air through her scented hankie.

'Lady Gretchen,' the duke called to the corridor. His bodyguards parted and a dour dame with a large horsehair bottom-warmer strode into the room wielding an ear trumpet. 'Lady Gretchen minded Prince Leo's father and me and our grandfather before that. Didn't you, Lady Gretchen?'

Lady Gretchen raised a bushy eyebrow, harrumphed, and dumped her well-padded bones onto a sofa in the corner. The queen looked helplessly at Olivia. 'We'll be back shortly,' she assured. 'Very shortly.'

Once the queen and the duke were down the turret stairs, Leo closed the door and pressed his back against it. He gave the princess a long once-over. She felt as if she'd forgotten to put on her dress. 'You're not as pretty as your picture.'

'Good,' Olivia said. 'Then you don't need to look at me.'

The prince curled his lip. Chunks of breakfast were stuck between his teeth. (*He's packed enough for a meal*, Olivia thought.) He wandered over to the window bars. 'Is that the witch's forest past the cornfields?'

'Yes.'

He grunted. 'My uncle says you're protected by an egg.'

'A pysanka,' Olivia corrected. 'It's coloured with special designs to ward off evil.'

'It's still an egg,' Leo sniffed. 'What a stupid charm. For *my* birthday, Father's wizard has promised me a cloak of invisibility.'

'Too bad you don't have it with you,' Olivia said sweetly. 'It would be nice to see you disappear.'

Leo paused. 'Was that supposed to be a joke?'

'Only if you found it funny.'

His eyes narrowed. 'Are you mocking me? Do you know who I am?'

'Yes,' Olivia tossed back. 'A very rude boy who looks at me in a way I don't appreciate.'

Leo sucked porridge from his molars. 'I expect my wife to be friendly.'

'What business is that of mine?'

'You don't know?' He laughed. 'We're to be married.'

'In your dreams. I'm to be a guest at your father's palace. That's all, unless *I* decide otherwise. And you're making my decision very easy.'

'Is that a fact?' Leo sauntered towards her. 'Listen well, little girl. From now on, I'm the one who makes your decisions. You're to be my wife. Yes, and you'll do what I want, or I'll have you locked in my father's dungeon next to my aunt.'

'You don't scare me,' Olivia said, moving quickly to the far side of the marble table. 'I'm telling Mother and Father what you said.'

'Who cares? What do you expect them to do about it? Your father's a vegetable. Your mother's a slap up from a chambermaid.'

'Get out of my room.'

'Make me.'

'Lady Gretchen!'

Lady Gretchen snored.

'Milady knows when to fall asleep,' Leo breathed heavily. 'It helps that she's deaf. Now show me some respect. Come here.'

'No.'

'No?' Leo began to circle the table. 'Here, kitty, kitty, kitty.'

Olivia scrambled to keep the table between them. 'Stay away. I'll scream for the guards.'

'Whose? My uncle and I have two hundred soldiers inside your courtyard. Your guards are outnumbered.' He lunged at her.

Olivia whipped a hairpin from her ringlets and swung wildly. The pin nicked Leo's cheek.

'You'll pay for that!' he yelped.

But before he could attack, Penelope leapt from Olivia's pocket and ran up his trouser leg. Leo hopped around the room, slapping at his legs. 'Ow! Ow!' he squealed as the little mouse nipped at his buttocks.

'Ready to leave?'

'Yes! Please! Anything! Make it stop!'

'Penelope, that will be all, thank you.'

Leo screamed as Penelope ran up his shirt and exited out through his collar. She jumped onto the table, and hopped back into Olivia's pocket.

Lady Gretchen blinked awake with a snort. 'What's going on?' she demanded sternly.

'Nothing. Prince Leo was just leaving,' Olivia said with a glare at the royal bully.

'It's been a lovely visit,' Leo snarled. 'But remember, Princess, your life depends on your pysanka. And I'll be carrying it to Pretonia.'

With that, he turned on his heel and marched out of the door, the gouty chaperone trailing after.

THE FAREWELL FEAST

Olivia's last meal in the castle was another kind of nightmare. Leo's uncle had assumed responsibility for her safety. 'No witch can best me or my men,' he'd boasted. 'At the evening meal, bring the girl to the dining hall. If the witch dares show her face, my men will send her to Hell!'

So Olivia sat at the great oak table between her mother and father, and opposite Prince Leo and his uncle. A hundred Pretonian soldiers lined the walls of the great hall, each with a counterfeit pysanka in a silver casing identical to Olivia's chained to his chest. The second hundred commanded security throughout the castle, bossing her parents' troops.

In honour of the castle's guests and Olivia's last supper at home, Queen Sophia had gone all out. Coronation banners embroidered with jewels hung from the rafters, while the walls were festooned with rivers of silk brocade. The table was anchored by silver candelabra representing fountains with dragons and mermaids, and by horns of plenty cascading with figs, dates, and pomegranates.

There were baskets of fine breads; a tureen of prawns in a sauce of creamed apricot and pear; a boar stuffed with sausages and walnuts; pheasants under glass; and a twenty-layer chocolate-and-butter-cream cake crammed with glazed cherries and plums.

Yet despite the festive flourishes, the freedom from her cell, and more company than she'd had in years, Olivia felt alone and desperate. To her left, her father sat motionless, his eyes full to bursting, his valet attempting to feed him without success. To her right, her mother's smile kept trembling into tears, and her hands shook so badly she could barely hold her cutlery. Tucked in her pocket, Penelope tried to comfort by gently kneading Olivia's leg with her little front paws.

Leo's uncle was ignorant of their pain. He amused the table – if that was the word – with loud tales of his valour, roared at his own jokes, and quaffed ale and wine in equal measure, pounding his tankard on the table for exclamation.

'So tomorrow's your birthday,' he bellowed at Olivia. 'Thirteen. A woman. And leaving home. Your heart in Pretonia – or with the Dream Witch!' The queen shuddered. The duke belched. 'Never fear. I've drowned a hundred witches in my time, and burned a hundred more.' So it continued.

Meanwhile, Prince Leo slouched opposite, his mouth hanging open. He lolled his tongue, dribbled food, and stared where he shouldn't. Olivia covered her top with her napkin and wrapped her feet behind her chair legs to keep them away from his roving toes. Oh, how she wished she could leap over the table and pop his pimples with her fork.

She knew she couldn't of course – couldn't even speak up about how he'd taunted her in her cell and tried to grab her. If she talked, her parents would have to do something. And the moment they did, Leo might seize the castle. He had the power, and knew it, too.

So Olivia sat quietly staring at her food as the duke droned on and Leo tormented her with his eyes. She glared at him. He smirked. It was intolerable.

After the meal, which ended when the duke passed out, Olivia returned to her cell with her mother and a troop of Pretonian guards. A dozen of the men formed a triple rank outside her door, while twenty more took up positions on the spiral staircase.

Olivia settled Penelope on the pillow next to her own and changed into her nightie. Meanwhile, her mother checked the closets and armoire to make sure no one had got into the room while they were out. 'You barely touched your meal,' she said, looking under the bed.

'I wasn't hungry. You didn't eat much either.'

'True, but you have a long journey ahead. You'll need your strength.' From the courtyard, the hoots and hollers of carousing soldiers broke the night air. The queen dusted off her hands and went to the window. 'I'll have Cook pack extra snacks. The sort of treats you like. Ginger biscuits. Tarts and marmalade.'

'It's all right,' Olivia said, dully. 'The duke's people eat well by the look of them.'

The queen looked into the starry night. 'A full moon,' she shivered, 'as big as a cauldron. At least we can see whatever's out there.' The soldiers below broke into a drinking song. Olivia's mother locked the shutters and turned to tuck her daughter in for the last time.

Olivia steadied her breath. *I mustn't let Mother know I'm afraid*, she thought.

Somehow her mother knew anyway; or knew that she herself was afraid. 'Shall I spend the night with you?'

Olivia wanted to say 'yes' more than anything in the world. But if her mother stayed, she knew that sooner or later she'd blurt out the truth about Leo. Then what? A battle with the prince? Or would she even be believed? Might her mother think she was making it up to stay at home? Or exaggerating a schoolboy tease? It was all too horrible to imagine.

Olivia twined her mother's fingers in her own. 'Thank you,' she said, 'but from now on I'm going to have to learn to take care of myself. What better way to start than to be alone tonight in my own room?'

'That's my brave girl,' her mother said. 'But if ever you want me, call the guards at once. I'll be just below, and here in an instant.' She kissed her gently and made her way to the cell door, eyes never leaving her daughter. 'Good night, dear heart.'

'Good night.'

Her mother blew her one last kiss and left, bolting the door behind her.

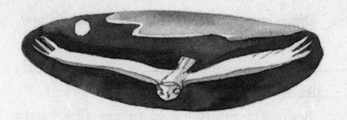

THE MOMENT OF TRUTH

The room was swallowed up by silence. Olivia fancied she could hear the shadows cast by her night lamp dancing on the walls.

She curled into a ball and turned to Penelope. 'What am I to do? I *can't* go with Leo. But I can't *not*.'

The little mouse peered in her eyes with such devotion that, for a moment, Olivia imagined she understood. *You can run away.*

'What?' Olivia sat up.

The little mouse scratched her muzzle with her front paws. *You can run away.*

Olivia's eyes bugged wide. 'Penelope?'

The mouse scrunched its nose.

'Don't tease me Penelope. Can you really talk, or am I crazy?'

Before the mouse could answer, there was a sharp tapping from inside the armoire near her bed.

Olivia leapt out of bed. 'Milo?'

'Yes. May I come in?'

'Just a minute.' Olivia ran to the wall of wardrobes on the far side of the room and scrambled into a pair of leggings.

Penelope stood on her hind legs. 'What are you doing?' This time her squeak was loud and clear.

'I *knew* you could talk,' Olivia said. She threw on a smock. 'If this isn't a dream, I'm running away.'

'Olivia, no!'

'Why not? You suggested it yourself.'

'Running away, yes. But not with him!'

'Why not? I'll be safer than on my own. I'll have my pysanka, too.' She whirled a dark hooded cloak around her shoulders.

'He'll try to break it.'

'Don't be silly.' She slipped on a pair of shoes.

'Believe me, he will! He will!'

'Fine.' Olivia rolled her eyes. 'I'll keep the pysanka hidden in my cloak if it makes you feel better. But I'm leaving: Milo can't be worse than Leo.'

'You've no idea,' Penelope wailed. She leapt from the bed and ran for the crack under the cell door.

'Where are you going?'

'To tell the guards. To raise the alarm!'

'Stop! To them you're a mouse. They'll stomp on you.'

Penelope froze. Olivia snatched her up and stared at her, nose to whiskers. 'You can come with me, or I can shut you up in a stocking drawer. But you won't stop me. Understood?'

'What to do, what to do,' the little mouse quivered.

Olivia slipped Penelope up her sleeve. Then she fetched the ribbon box from its lower shelf in her closets and retrieved the last pysanka safe in its silver shell. She put it in the lining pocket of her cloak and opened the armoire door.

Milo stayed in the cupboard's shadows. Olivia saw bruises on his arm and cheek; one of his eyes was swollen.

'Milo,' she gasped. 'What happened?'

Milo shrank from the lamplight. 'I fell.'

Penelope poked her head out of Olivia's sleeve: 'That's a lie. You're part of a trap. Last night, she beat you when you came back empty-handed, didn't she?'

'No!' Milo exclaimed and turned his head away.

'Tell the princess the truth,' Penelope pleaded.

'I can't.'

Olivia stepped back. 'Who's she? What's so bad you can't tell?'

'No one. Nothing.'

Olivia frowned. 'You appear out of thin air, beaten and bruised; you talk to a mouse. Most people would find that strange – not you. So let's start there. If this isn't a dream, what is it?'

'You don't know what you're asking.'

'I do so. What I *don't* know is what you're hiding.'

Milo was torn by fear and shame. He rubbed his hands. 'How can I say it?'

'You have a good heart,' Penelope said. 'I can see it in your eyes. Say what it tells you.'

Milo looked from the mouse to Olivia and back again. Then he took a deep breath and dropped to his knees before the princess. 'Forgive me.'

'For what?'

'For what I came to do. She said she'd kill me if I didn't help her. She said my parents would never see me again. She said they'd die of grief.'

'Who's *she*?'

'The Dream Witch. I'm her prisoner. She said if I brought you to her lair, she'd set me free. But that's a lie. I'd never be free. I'd have nightmares as long as I lived.'

Olivia frowned. 'How did the witch get you

75

into the armoire? No, wait, don't tell me,' she exclaimed. 'She put you inside the picture of the cottage with the picket fence.'

Milo nodded. 'The witch sends people to the places she draws on parchments of bat wings; she calls them portals. Only she didn't know how to draw the inside of your turret. That's why she had her owl, Doomsday, fly me to your window in the picture of her cottage. That picture is the portal to travel back and forth to her lair.'

Olivia's head swam. 'I thought the picture of her cottage was a dream-drawing because the chimney smoke drifted off the parchment. But it was real.'

'Yes,' Milo said. 'Only you weren't paying attention. That was no picket fence.' He picked up the parchment and held it to her face.

Olivia fell back, her hand over her mouth. As she'd remembered, the thatching of the cottage was like hair, and the windows like eyes. But the picket fence was made of thighbones each capped by a skull. The door was lined with teeth. And the smoke from the chimney smelled of burning flesh.

'I was sent to bring you to her. But I won't. I can't.' He threw the parchment back on the armoire floor and looked at Olivia in terror. 'What will become of us now?'

TRAPPED

Milo didn't have to wait long to find out.

Without warning, the queen threw open the cell door. Guards stormed in followed by Leo and his bleary-eyed uncle. They dragged Milo out of the closet and threw him down in the centre of the room.

'We caught you this time, Demon!' the queen exclaimed. 'You're in thrall to the Dream Witch, aren't you? What enchantment did you place on my daughter? Why is she in a hooded cape?'

'That's *my* doing, Mother,' Olivia piped up. 'His name is Milo. He's a boy from the country.

He doesn't mean any harm.'

'A peasant in the castle?' Leo yelled. 'I'll have his head.' He drew his sword.

The duke grabbed Leo's arm. 'All in good time. First, let's learn what the knave knows. The lash and the thumbscrew will loosen his tongue.'

'Leave him alone,' Olivia blurted. 'I asked him here to help me run away.'

'Why?' her mother asked, astonished. 'You're protected by our guests.'

'I'm no more safe with Leo than with the witch. Ask him what he said to me when you left us alone. Ask him what he tried to do.'

Leo's blotches bubbled red. 'I never said or tried to do anything.'

'Liar! You said I'd be forced into marriage and made to obey you.'

The duke blinked in fury. 'Teach your girl some manners, Highness.'

Queen Sophia cupped Olivia's head in her hands. She saw the pain and fear in her eyes. She turned to Leo and his uncle. 'Excellencies, you are our honoured guests, but I rule this kingdom in my husband's stead. I shall speak to the boy and render justice as I see fit. As for my daughter: If she enters your protection, it will be as a guest, not a prize.'

The duke's eyelid twitched: 'Wrong on both counts, Highness. The prisoner has challenged the honour of the Pretonian court: We will decide his fate. As for the princess, she may be free to refuse Prince Leo but only a madwoman or a witch would make such a choice. For those, we have the asylum and the stake.'

'How dare you!' the queen exclaimed. 'You and your men will be gone by sunrise.'

'No. The girl's mine.' Leo stomped his foot. 'I want her and I'll have her! Father said I could.'

'Your father doesn't own me,' Olivia snapped. 'Neither do you.'

The duke's voice went dark as a dungeon: 'We haven't come this far to go home empty-handed. You made a pact. It shall be honoured.' He raised his hand; his soldiers drew their weapons. The queen clutched Olivia tight.

'Did you think the girl's protection came free?' the duke continued. 'She'll inherit this kingdom on your husband's death. Her marriage will give Pretonia your fields for our granaries and your forests for our sport.'

'And I shall call you "Mother",' Leo smirked at the queen.

Queen Sophia threw back her shoulders. 'I'll have no brat like you.'

The duke laughed and pressed his blade to Milo's throat. 'Now, boy. What's that drawing on the floor beside you?'

'A portal to the Dream Witch.'

The duke speared it with his sword and held it to the lamp light. The parchment shrieked and burst into flames. Outside, a greater shriek rent the night. A blast of wind rattled the shutters. The bolt popped free. The shutters crashed open against the stone walls. Through the window, Olivia saw a blaze shoot up from the middle of the forest.

The fiery parchment flapped its sides. It flew off the sword and around the room. Thunder rumbled beyond. Rain poured onto the fire in the forest. The flames fizzled, both in the woods and on the drawing. A plume of smoke rose into the night; the charred portal swooped away through the window bars.

Then, without warning, the Dream Witch flew up from the forest on her giant cleaver. She hurtled towards the castle, silhouetted against the moon. Slicing through the sky, cutting above the cornfields and town, it looked like she'd crash through the window bars.

Everyone dropped to the floor. But at the last second, the witch yanked the cleaver's mighty handle, and sheared to a powerful parallel stop, rearing her trunk in anger.

'You dare try to destroy me, Queen?' she shrieked, hovering outside the turret. 'You who came to me with a dream and a promise?' Smoke shot from her nostrils.

'Dream Witch, no. I've only tried to protect my daughter.'

'Ha! You sought to burn me in my lair. Consider us at war. In the underworld beneath my cottage is a chamber of children, kidnapped because you wouldn't pay your debt. Surrender the princess by dawn, or I'll grind them to dust.'

The witch's words echoed over the countryside. Wails pierced the night air. Howls of: 'Why *our* children? Why not yours?' 'Why not one child instead of a hundred?'

'Hear the cries of your people,' the witch warned, 'or their grief shall tear your castle apart.'

'Silence witch,' the duke commanded. 'The girl belongs to us. With her, we hold the keys to this kingdom. If peasants attack this castle we'll slaughter them.' He hollered down to the courtyard: 'Archers. Send the witch on her way.'

His men shot up a volley of arrows. The Dream Witch swung her trunk. The arrows turned in mid air and rained back at the soldiers.

'As for you, Milo my boy,' the witch cackled over the screams below, 'your parents shall never see you again. And you, Princess, by dawn, I shall have your heart in my hand.' She reared her cleaver and tore back through the sky to her lair.

The duke whirled on the queen. 'You're the author of this misfortune. You and your husband have ruled with a weak hand. Why else would a witch feel free to challenge you? Fear is the heart of power. Your meekness has bred licence.'

'And your brutishness, hatred!' Olivia spoke out.

The duke swatted her with the back of his hand. She fell to the floor. Her mother ran to her with a cry.

'You'll learn to hold your tongue, girl. You'll teach her, won't you, Nephew?'

'With pleasure,' Leo leered.

The duke ripped the key to the cell from the queen's neck and gave it to the prince. He turned to his men. 'Lock her Highness in her bedchamber and disarm her troops. Then throw this boy in the dungeon.'

The soldiers left on their mission.

'Mother! Milo!' Olivia called out as they were dragged away, 'I'll find a way to save you.'

Leo turned at the door. 'You can't even save yourself.'

THE TALE OF A TAIL

Olivia ran towards the cell door. It slammed in her face. She reeled backwards. 'What shall I do?'

'Take a deep breath,' Penelope said. 'All is not lost. Trust me.'

The princess slumped on her bed. Penelope scampered onto the pillow beside her and wagged a paw.

'Listen well and I'll tell you a tale of a tail. My tale. Once upon a time, in the days when fear could be managed with a cup of cocoa, a princess was born who was destined to save her kingdom. Her family had a wizard named

Ephemia who gave her a dozen pysanka to protect her from danger. But no sooner were the
talismans in her cradle than the Dream Witch
arrived to take her heart.'

'I know this story,' Olivia said. 'It's the story
of my christening.'

'Ah, but you don't know the ending.'

'I do so. The good Ephemia raised her wand.
But instead of destroying the evil one, she herself was destroyed and vanished in a puff of
smoke.'

Penelope stroked her whiskers. 'That's what
people *think* they saw. But in all the confusion,
when the smoke cleared, no one noticed the
little grey mouse quivering under the baby's
pram.'

Olivia's eyes went wide. 'Penelope! You're
Ephemia!'

'Indeed,' Ephemia replied. 'I mixed up my
spell words and turned myself into a mouse.
For nearly thirteen years I've kept my secret.
I've been able to watch over my little princess,
while slipping unnoticed from the gaze of the

Dream Witch and her familiars. Still, there've been times I've had to bite my tail. Being stuck in drawers is no life for a wizard. It's a good thing I like cheese.'

'Penelope, I'm sorry.'

'Penelope. That's another thing. What kind of name is Penelope?'

'It's no worse than Ephemia.'

'That depends in which century you grew up,' the wizard sniffed. 'At any rate, from now on, call me Ephemia, please.'

'Of course,' Olivia said. 'But what's your plan? We're losing time. Mother and Father are in danger, Milo is facing torture, and by dawn the Dream Witch swears to have my heart or grind up the kingdom's children.'

'I'm not *that* forgetful,' Ephemia said. 'Your parents are safe for now. The immediate danger is to that young man. To the dungeon, then, and from there, to the witch's lair in the world beneath her cottage. Along the way, I'll tell you what you must do to rescue the kingdom's children by dawn.'

'Why don't you just cast some spells?'

Ephemia covered her head with her paws. 'I'm finished with spells, my girl. Oh yes, I learned my lesson on your christening day. With my luck, I might turn you into a bean sprout.'

'But without magic, how can we do *anything*?'

'Oh, I've still got some tricks,' Ephemia winked. 'There are burrows from the forest floor into the witch's caverns. Being a mouse, I can speak to woodland creatures. They can help us.'

'Yes, but what use is their help now? We're locked in a cell.'

Ephemia winked. 'There's a loose plank under your bed with a knothole at one end. Lift the plank and drop down into the secret passageway that leads through the castle.'

'A secret passageway?' Olivia dived under her bed.

'Well, secret to humans, anyway. There's not a castle nook nor cranny unknown to spiders, mice, and squirrels.'

Olivia found the plank. 'What a crazy place for an entrance.'

'Where would you put it?'

'On a wall of course.' Olivia stuck her finger in the knothole. 'I'd put it behind a painting, or a swinging fireplace, or a wall of books.'

'Right where everyone would think to look? Now that's what *I* call crazy.'

Olivia removed the plank and peered down. The passage floor was only two feet below. 'This isn't a passageway,' Olivia exclaimed. 'It's a crawl space.'

'Not to me,' Ephemia said.

'You're a mouse. I'm a princess.'

'With an attitude like that you'll never survive the Dream Witch,' Ephemia sniffed. 'Come. You may not be able to stand, but you can wriggle.'

Olivia looked doubtfully into the dark beneath. 'How am I to see?'

'I'll guide you,' Ephemia hopped into the hole. 'Don't worry, my pet. My little mouse eyes can see in the dark. Besides, I know these walls backwards.'

Olivia imagined herself stuck in the stone-work, entombed forever in the unforgiving castle walls. But she knew she had no choice. She took a deep breath and squeezed down into the musty crawl space.

TO THE DUNGEON

'The crawl space is open as far as the outer wall of the turret stairs,' Ephemia said.

Thank heavens, Olivia thought, as she wormed her way through the dark.

Ephemia had promised clear passage, but it was a surprisingly winding route. 'A little to the left, Princess.'

'Why? What's on the right?'

'A dead rat, poor thing. Remember the smell a year ago at Easter? He's all dried up now. Still, not very pleasant.'

'Ew. And what are these bits of something under my hands?'

'Grape seeds.'

'Grape seeds?'

'Ask me no questions, I'll tell you no lies.'

Olivia bumped her head into something hard.

'Sorry,' Ephemia said. 'I forgot about the support pillars. There's a second one to your right. Squeeze between them. We're about to go under the wall of your cell.'

Olivia wriggled through the opening. The floorboards creaked over her head as the soldiers above paced in front of her cell door.

Ephemia nuzzled her nose to Olivia's ear. 'Crawl forward till you hit the back of the top step of the staircase.'

Olivia felt her way to the riser. 'What now?'

'To your left, there's a gap between the crawl space and the stairs. It opens onto a perilous drop to the castle's foundations.'

'You want me to plummet to the dungeon?'

'No. I want you to climb down the support beams beside the staircase. A word to the wise: Don't look down.'

'Why not? I can't see anyway.'

'Lucky you.'

Olivia wriggled to the opening and swung her legs over the void. With one hand, she touched the outer wall of the staircase. With her feet, she found the first support beam and eased herself down.

'Excellent. Now squat down, grab the beam, and drop your legs as far as they'll go. Your feet will be just above the next support.'

Olivia took hold of the beam and let her legs dangle. Her toe landed on a brick abandoned by the castle's builders. It slid off the support and hurtled to the ground below. Olivia tried not to scream.

'It's all right,' Ephemia squeaked. 'You're right above the beam. Just let yourself go.'

'I can't.'

'You can.'

Olivia gulped. She dropped onto the beam and held out her arms to steady herself. One hand touched the outer wall of the staircase. She pressed her fingers against its cool, damp surface.

Something ran over her toes. 'Ephemia?'

'Yes?' The mouse was above her.

'Ephemia . . . if you're up there . . . what's at my feet?'

'A rat.'

'A rat?' Olivia gasped.

'A little one,' Ephemia replied airily. 'Don't worry, it's run off. You scared it.'

'*I* scared *it*?'

'Stop being a silly goose. You've work to do. Sit down on the support.'

'I don't think I can do anything right now.'

'Suit yourself. But there's a large hairy spider about to crawl on your fingers.'

In an instant, Olivia was perched on the support. Ephemia coached from her shoulder, as the princess lowered herself to the next beam, and the one after that and the one after that and the one after that. Her cloak nearly tripped her, but she soon learned to keep it looped over an arm. Soon the beams felt like rungs on a ladder; haphazard and far apart, but rungs nonetheless.

On the other side of the staircase wall, she

could hear the life of the castle. It seemed to come from far away, like what she'd heard when she was little and stuck her head in the courtyard rain barrel. She tried to hear and not hear at the same time – eager and afraid to know what was happening. The clomping on the stairs, the rumble of voices – what were they about? Had Leo found her missing? Was there news about her parents?

Ephemia read her mind. 'What's happening there is happening there. Keep your mind on the here and now, or you'll tumble down and have nothing to think about ever.'

Olivia concentrated hard. *One step at a time. One step at a time.* Before she knew it, what had seemed impossible had become real. She'd reached a dingy alcove above two squat pillars, eight feet from the dungeon floor.

Olivia shivered. Before she'd been locked away, she'd played hide-and-seek in the cells with the servants' children. One day, she'd nearly tripped into an open well. Her parents were horrified. They said she'd have disappeared into the underground river that ran beneath the castle.

Ephemia saw Olivia's hesitation. 'There's only one way down.'

Olivia said a prayer, hung from the alcove, and dropped into the dungeon.

FLIGHT INTO DANGER

She landed softly, Ephemia on her shoulder. The air was ripe with decay. The only light was a torch the Pretonians had set at the foot of the staircase. Shadows flickered over a maze of narrow Gothic archways.

Olivia pressed herself against the pillar by the stairs. From somewhere in the gloom, she heard a muffled rush of river water echoing up the well, and farther off, the growls of Milo's guards. She turned her nose to Ephemia. 'We'll never get to Milo. Even if we do, we'll never escape alive.'

'Buck up. I'm the mouse, not you.'

'I can't help it. I'm scared.'

'Who isn't? Courage isn't feeling brave. It's fighting fear.'

'How?'

'A dose of pretend never hurt.'

True or not, Olivia determined to try. She imagined herself a warrior princess and threw back her shoulders. 'Let's go.'

'That's my girl,' Ephemia said. She jumped off Olivia's cloak and scampered down the passage leading from the stairs. 'I'll scout ahead,' she said and disappeared through a crevice in the bricks.

Olivia peered down the empty hall. In the distance, a second torch lit another corridor – a signpost leading to the voices of the guards. She darted from archway to archway, past banks of fetid cells. Olivia imagined prisoners from centuries past, cutthroats and villains, reaching out for her through the gloom. She raced all the faster.

Soon she was at the crossway. By the sound of the river water, the well was nearby; beyond it, Milo and the guards.

'Speak up, boy,' a voice yelled, 'where do you live?'

'I forget.'

Smack.

Olivia peeked around the pillar. Milo was past the last archway. He was faced away from her, on a stool in an open cavern. His hands were tied behind his back. A blazing fire pit was at his feet. Six ruffians in chainmail circled him, their hairy faces glistening in the fire's heat.

'Who are your ma and pa?'

'The ones who raised me.'

Smack. 'Their names! Where do they live?'

'Hit me all you like. I'll never betray them.'

Olivia's throat went dry. Where was Ephemia? What was she to do?

A beefy guard grabbed Milo by the chest and head. Another raised a pair of pliers. 'Talk, boy, or you'll never talk again.'

Olivia could bear it no longer. She leapt into the corridor. 'Stop!'

The guards whirled around.

There was no turning back. Olivia, warrior

princess, skirted the well hole and marched past the last row of cells into the cavern.

'Who are you?' demanded the beefiest brute.

'The princess Olivia,' she said boldly, 'soon to be wife of your prince and one day queen of Pretonia.'

The guard glanced at her trousers and cloak. 'Curious clothes for a princess.'

Olivia thrust her nose in the air. 'Silly man. We are disguised for our journey. Were none of you in the turret when this rascal was captured? You'd have seen me, then.'

The guard with the pliers stepped forward. 'Oh, I was there. An' I seen you all right. Put under lock and key by the duke and the prince himself.'

'Was I indeed? Then what, pray, am I doing here?'

The man spat. 'That's what I'd like to know.'

'Since when is it the business of a wretch like you to know the affairs of his betters?'

The man frowned. 'I know what I seen is all.'

'Fool!' Olivia turned to the other guards.

'Does this idiot suppose I waltzed down a stairwell of soldiers without Prince Leo's say-so? Or does he think I vanished into thin air and appeared before you out of pixie dust?'

The guards laughed nervously.

Olivia fixed an imperious gaze on her questioner. 'What is your name, sirrah? His Excellency shall hear of your impertinence. If I have my way, we'll march to Pretonia with your head on a pike!'

The man looked to his friends in confusion. They stared at their feet. Finding himself alone, he dropped the pliers and fell to his knees. 'Beg pardon, Your Highness. My name is Gunther. I meant no harm. What does Your Highness want?'

'Much better,' Olivia declared grandly. 'If you must know, I'd have a word with the miscreant who dared enter my chamber.' She took a red-hot poker from the fire pit and pointed it at Milo. 'Give us twenty paces and turn your backs. What I am about to do may distress you.'

The men could scarcely believe their ears but only a fool would risk his head for twenty paces. They retreated to the edge of the cavern and turned away.

'You, peasant boy! You, varlet!' Olivia declaimed to Milo. 'May your flesh sizzle for your sins!'

Milo's eyes went big as saucepans. 'What?'

Olivia winked, dropped to her knees, and began to untie his hands. 'I'm helping you escape,' she whispered. 'Now scream. Or do I have to use the poker for real?'

Milo screamed.

'Yes, scream, scurvy knave!' Olivia roared theatrically as the knots loosened. 'Take this brand for entering my room!'

Milo screamed again.

'This for speaking my name.'

He screamed again.

'And this for stealing my brass candlesticks!'

'Brass candlesticks?' Milo mouthed.

'All I could think of,' Olivia shrugged, as she removed the cords. 'Keep screaming.'

But Milo was suddenly too frightened to scream.

'What's the matter?'

'Guess.' It was Prince Leo.

Olivia looked up with a start. Leo's men spun to attention.

'What's the meaning of this?' the prince demanded of the guards. 'Seize the prisoners.'

Milo sprang to his feet. But before he and Olivia could run, the guards grabbed them tight.

'You thought to escape with that peasant?' Leo raged at Olivia. 'Watch, as I sever him limb from limb!'

'No!' Olivia cried.

Four guards pinned Milo to the floor. 'Try running with no legs,' Leo taunted. He raised his sword above his head.

At that moment, an otherworldly wail echoed from a cell down the corridor. 'You, Leopold, Prince of Pretonia! You dare awaken the dungeon dead?' It was a voice, ancient and crazed; the voice of a ghostly crone.

Leo froze. 'Who's there?'

'The Headless Hunchback of Horning. Beheaded in this dungeon five hundred years ago.'

'How do I know this isn't a trick?'

'You don't,' the ghost said darkly.

Leo turned to the nearest guard. 'G-go. S-see who or what it is.'

The guard took a lantern and edged towards the cell, dagger at the ready. He peered between the bars: 'There's no one there.'

'No one?' the ghost cackled. A rusty tin cup rolled out of the shadows.

The guard jumped and ran back screaming.

'What do you want, demon?' Leo trembled.

'Company, my lovey. We ghosties need new dead for our games. New dead to haunt these halls.'

'Not us. Please,' Leo begged. 'We're strangers to this court. This girl here, take her and her friend. She's princess of this castle.'

'No, my little weasel. It's you we want!' The voice was above his head.

Leo shrieked, clattered down the corridors,

and raced up the dungeon stairs, his terrified guards howling at his heels.

'So they've left you to my mercy,' the ghost gloated.

'Ephemia, stop it,' Olivia sighed. 'You had me scared to death. What took you so long?'

The little mouse waltzed onto the overhead beam. 'I like to make an entrance.'

'So what do we do now?' Milo asked. 'There's no way out.'

Ephemia raised a paw. 'Actually there is.'

'What? Where?' Olivia asked, and instantly knew the answer. 'Oh no.'

'Oh yes.'

Olivia turned and faced the well.

DOWN THE CHUTE

Olivia and Milo looked down the well hole. It was a ten-foot jump into the dark, rushing waters beneath.

'At the foot of castle hill, the river empties into the great marsh on the outskirts of town,' Ephemia said.

'It can empty into the ocean for all I care,' Olivia replied. 'I can't swim.'

'Neither can I,' Milo piped up.

'Not to worry,' Ephemia assured them. 'Just curl into a ball and hold your breath. The river will carry you to your destination.'

'But . . .'

'But me no buts. Would you rather wait till Leo's uncle storms down with a hundred of his soldiers? Drowning's the least of your worries.'

Olivia gazed into the unforgiving roar. Pretending to be a warrior princess was harder than it seemed. She whirled the cloak from her shoulders and rolled it into a ball, so it wouldn't snag on a root and drown her.

'Tuck the cloak into your middle and hold tight,' Ephemia said. 'The pysanka case is safe in its pocket, but take care it doesn't fall out in the river's rush.' She stood on her hind legs. 'Right, then. Last one in and so forth.' She leapt into the well and disappeared in the racing current.

Milo glanced at Olivia. 'If we don't survive, thank you for saving me from those guards. This is a much better way to die.'

'You're welcome.' Olivia clutched her bundle of cloak. 'And thank *you* for . . .' She suddenly realised she had nothing to thank Milo for at all. But it seemed rude to say so, so instead she said, 'Thank you for being nice.'

And jumped.

Olivia heard the rush, the splash. Then silence as she plunged beneath the surface. She felt herself spun around, tumbled, carried far from the well. Where was up? Down?

For a second, her head bobbed above the water. She gulped a breath. The world was black as pitch – and cold and wet and –

'Milo?'

Her cry was lost in the din. The current pulled her back under. Sucked her down feet first. Or was she falling? Spinning down underground rapids?

Water shot up Olivia's nose. She coughed, gagged – and suddenly was spewed into an underground pool. Where? Some place where the torrent slowed at least. She sank beneath the surface and touched bottom with her toes. Pushing off, she bobbed forward.

The water was now no deeper than her neck. Good. She hadn't drowned. Yet. She thrashed forward. Soon, the water was down to her waist.

But where to go now? 'Hello?' she called out.

'Olivia?'

'Ephemia?'

'I'm over here, on top of a boulder,' the mouse said. 'I can see starlight on the water ahead. It's the mouth of the marsh.'

'Where's Milo?'

'Whoah!' There was a splash behind her as Milo shot into the pool.

'Milo, over here, it's shallow,' Olivia called out. 'Follow my voice. Ephemia's found the way out.'

Olivia waded towards her guardian. By the glimmer of light, she saw the silhouette of Ephemia's rock where it broke the surface. When she reached it, she put down a hand. Ephemia scurried to her shoulder.

Milo joined them. 'We made it.'

'What did I tell you?' Ephemia tsked.

They sloshed their way to the opening, a low overhang of rock and root. Bulrushes grew along the outer banks. Forging through, they scrambled onto muddy ground.

'I need to get home, let Mama and Papa know I'm all right,' Milo said. 'Come with me. You can hide with my family. The soldiers don't know where I live.'

'The Dream Witch does,' Ephemia said, shaking the wet from her haunches. 'Lead us to your house. I'll check if she's lurking. When I give the all-clear, you and your parents must flee.'

'And you with us.'

'No,' Olivia said. 'Ephemia and I have to head to the forest. I need to face the Dream Witch by dawn.'

'She'll kill you.'

'Better that than her grinding up the kingdom's children. I'm the reason they're in trouble.'

'I should go with you.'

'No,' Olivia shook her head. 'I won't put anyone else in danger. Besides, you need to be with your parents. They've already lost you once. I wouldn't have them grieve twice.'

'My home's in the cornfields near the forest,'

Milo said softly. 'Mama and Papa can give you some food.'

'Food.' Ephemia rubbed her paws. 'What are we waiting for?'

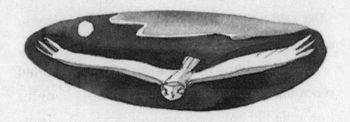

REUNION

Milo led them to the far side of the marsh. From there, they crept along the ditches that led to his family's home. Starlight lit the shapes of fields and fences, but Milo's feet knew the way. The nearer they got, the faster he went; soon he was running. 'It's just over that hill.' He and Olivia laid low as Ephemia scouted through thistles and brambles to the hill's crest. She ran back.

'Is the Dream Witch near?' Olivia whispered.

'No.' Ephemia wrung her tail. 'But Milo. Oh, Milo, I'm sorry.'

'What do you mean you're sorry?'

Ephemia could say no more.

Milo dashed up the hill. A faint breeze carried the scent of burnt wood and straw. Where his home had been was a smouldering ruin. To its left, he could see his mama and papa huddled together by a small campfire.

Milo bolted to his yard, followed closely by Olivia. At the sound of their approach, his mother scrambled to her feet.

'Who's there?'

'Me. It's me.' Milo ran inside the gate.

His father raised a pitchfork. 'Stay back.'

'Papa?' Milo froze in confusion.

'Who are you? Why are you calling me calling "Papa"?'

'Don't you recognise me?'

'Why should we?' his mother demanded. 'There's none but fiends and ruffians loose at this hour. Which are you? What do you want?'

'I don't want anything,' Milo gasped. 'Just to be with you.'

'Why? Can't you see we've nothing? We've lost our boy, our home, our everything. If you have any decency, leave us to our grief.'

'But Mama, Papa, it's Milo!'

His father's tears glistened in the firelight. 'How dare you taunt us? Our boy is gone forever.'

Milo trembled. *Your parents will never see you again*, the Dream Witch had said. It was true. Their eyes saw a stranger.

'Despair is her mightiest spell,' Ephemia murmured from the grasses. 'You'll never break it.'

Still, Milo tried: 'What would you do if I said you've been bewitched? That the Dream Witch has blinded you with pain.'

Milo's father gripped his pitchfork. 'I'd slay you for being the cruellest thief who ever lived: A thief who'd use our love for our dead son to gain our trust.'

Olivia stepped forward. 'Milo is alive, no matter what you think. You mustn't give up hope. That's what the Dream Witch wants you to do.'

His mother peered hard. 'And who are you?'

Olivia hesitated. Who'd believe a muddy girl was their princess? Worse, what might they do if they knew her as the reason the Dream Witch stole their child? 'I'm a friend of your son.'

'So am I,' Milo said. 'I was with him in the witch's cavern.'

'You lie, the pair of you,' Milo's mother exclaimed. 'We've never seen either one of you before. As for you, rascal, how could you be in that devil's den and live to tell the tale?'

'By luck, by grace. Call it what you will, but here I am,' Milo answered. 'And I swear to you, your son is in my head even as we speak. The words, "Mama, Papa, it's Milo," are his.'

Milo's father turned his pitchfork from one to the other. 'So now you claim to be a conjurer? Why should we trust you?'

'Because I know things only Milo could know.' Milo nodded to his father. 'The last time you saw him, you were whittling a bird from a piece of birch wood.' He nodded to his mother. 'You were peeling potatoes.'

His father's pitchfork dropped to the ground. 'You know!'

'And more besides. Milo was storming off to the cornfields. You begged him not to go. He wouldn't listen. And he said a terrible thing. He said he wished to run away and never see you or this place again.' Milo's voice grew thin. 'It wasn't true. But he said it. And now it's too late to unsay it. And he wants you to know he's sorry, *so* sorry, for all the pain he's caused you.'

'No pain, never pain,' his father said. 'Our boy brought us nothing but joy. It was our fault. We were too hard. We wouldn't listen. Oh, if he were only with us now, everything would be different.'

'You say you were together in the witch's cavern,' his mother whispered. 'Is he all right? Did he escape, too?'

'Yes,' Milo nodded. 'We fled together.'

'Where is he now?'

Milo waved his arms helplessly. 'As near as breath, as far away as happiness.'

'Don't torture us with riddles,' his father

pleaded. 'We have to see him. Take us to where he's hiding. Please.'

'I can't. I don't know how. All I know is that he loves you. He loves you more than anything.' Milo began to cry. His mother went to him and held him tight, and for a moment he felt safe and home again.

'There, there.' She stroked his hair. 'Why, you're wet and cold. You'll be catching your deaths of pneumonia, the pair of you. Come by our fire and dry yourselves. Friends of our son are like our own.' She brought them into the warmth.

'The night our boy was taken, we went to the forest to smoke the Dream Witch from her lair,' Milo's father said. 'But the moment our torches touched the trees, she burned our home to the ground.' He opened a bundle. 'Neighbours gave us some food and these clothes. Take them.'

'We can't,' Milo said.

'Please. Giving them to you will be like giving them to Milo.'

His mother held up a blanket for Olivia; his father held up one for him. Soon the pair were dried and dressed: Olivia in a cotton frock; Milo in a shirt and breeches; both with rough woollen capes and new boots.

Milo's mother gave them milk and corn bread. She couldn't abide mice, but had to smile at the sight of Olivia feeding crumbs to the tiny rodent at her feet. 'You'll stay the night?' she asked. 'Our son is gone, but while you're with us it's a little like he's here.'

'Thanks for your kindness,' Olivia said. 'But I must go. I've much to do before I sleep.'

Milo's eyes welled. 'I have to go, too. If the Dream Witch finds me here, who knows what she'll do to you.'

'There's nothing more she *can* do,' his mother said.

Milo hugged his parents goodbye. 'Your son wants you to know that he'll be fine. You're not to worry.'

'True or not, it's kind of you to say,' his father said.

'Why not come with us?' Milo blurted. 'We could keep each other safe. You could be my parents. I could be your son.'

'And what if our boy came home at last to find us gone? What then?'

'But what if he can't come home, not ever?'

'Then he'll be with us, still, in memory,' his mother said. 'This is the place where Milo was born; the place he first saw first dawn. He's in the air we breathe. Oh, lad, we'll never leave this place. No. Nor eat, nor sleep, until our boy is back or we have joined him on the other side.'

His father patted him on the back. 'Safe journey lad.'

'Peace be with you,' his mother said.

Olivia led Milo through the gate and away from his home.

Milo shuddered.

'Don't look back,' Olivia whispered. 'Don't look back.'

MEANWHILE, IN THE DUNGEON

Back at the castle, the Duke of Fettwurst was marching a parade of soldiers along the dungeon corridors; Prince Leo ran at his heels. The pounding of the soldiers' iron boots shook the dank air; the walls shivered under the flickering torchlight.

The duke strode past the well into the torture chamber. He turned to his nephew and stomped his foot. The company halted.

'This is the last place you saw the princess and the knave?'

'Yes, Uncle.'

'And it was here you encountered the ghost?'

'Yes. The Headless Hunchback of Horning. She was in that cell just past the well.'

'She?' His uncle frowned. 'You fled the dungeon because of a She?'

'We didn't flee,' Leo exclaimed indignantly. 'We went for reinforcements.'

'Because of a SHE???'

'A she, a he, I don't know,' Leo stammered.

'Can't you tell the difference?'

'The ghost didn't show itself.'

'Then how did it manifest?'

'It howled,' Leo said. 'And I think it cackled. Yes, it had a definite cackle.'

'What else? Did it toss things around or make a terrible whirlwind.'

'No,' Leo admitted. 'But it rolled a tin cup.'

The duke's eyelid twitched. 'It rolled a tin cup?'

'Yes. From the back of the cell,' Leo added helpfully. 'The torturers screamed.'

'Oh they did, did they? Where are those cowards? I'll give them something to scream about.'

'Uncle, it was very frightening.'

'A rolling cup frightening? I've seen scarier sights in a sausage shop!'

'It said it wanted new dead for its dungeon games.'

'Did it indeed.' The duke stormed to the ghost's cell and banged his armoured fist against the bars. 'Hear me, Headless Hunchback of Horning,' he bellowed. 'I'll find your rotted skull and use it to bowl ten-pins. Show yourself, now, if you dare.'

The dungeon was quiet as a bat blink.

The duke glared at Leo. 'That's how you tame a ghost.'

The soldiers applauded. The duke bowed. Leo blushed.

'But while we've lost a ghost,' the duke said coldly, 'we've lost the princess and our prisoner, too. Where are they? Who was guarding the top of the dungeon stairs?'

'We four, your Grace,' said a stalwart brute. He pointed to his comrades. 'We never seen the princess come down nor up.'

Leo shivered. 'Maybe she made herself invisible. Maybe she's a demon.'

'And maybe I'm a newt,' his uncle snorted. 'No. There must be another way out. A secret passageway in the walls. A trap door in the floor or ceiling.' He paused, and suddenly became aware of the sound of rushing water. He stared at the well. 'Of course! The answer is under our noses. The vixen and the boy jumped down the well and were carried away by the river.'

A soldier peered down the hole. 'But where does it empty?'

'Tell me when you find out,' the duke said and gave him a push.

There was a scream and a splash.

The duke put a hand on Prince Leo's shoulder. 'I'll stay here to keep the castle secure. As for you, Nephew, take fifty men and hunt down your damsel.'

THE WAYS OF THE WITCH

Milo's home was now a memory tucked behind the last hill. He found it hard to breathe. If he turned to Olivia and her mouse, or said a word, he knew he'd fall apart. So he stared straight ahead and let his wobbly legs carry him forward.

Olivia squeezed his arm. 'Your parents will be all right.'

Milo pulled away. 'No they won't. They'll pine away and die like the Dream Witch said. Even if I stay with them, that won't change. They'll never know who I am. I'm a stranger to them, and always will be.' He bent over and gripped his knees, then sank to the ground, gulping air.

Olivia knelt beside him. She waited till he went still. 'What are you going to do?' she asked quietly. 'Where are you going to go?'

Milo took a long, steady breath. 'I'm going with you to fight the Dream Witch.'

'You mustn't,' Olivia cautioned. 'There's no reason both of us should risk our lives.'

'My parents are dying because of me. How can I live knowing that? If we can defeat the Dream Witch, maybe her spells will be broken. Maybe I can save them.'

It was true. Olivia knew it. She took his hands. 'Let's make a vow, then. Let's promise ourselves that no matter how scared we get, we'll always remember there's someone else who's just as scared. We're not alone.'

'I'll say you're not,' Ephemia declared. 'As long as these little lungs have breath, you've a guardian, loyal and true.'

'The best in the world,' Olivia said. She picked up her furry companion. 'Back at the castle you said you knew the ways of the Dream Witch. Tell us, please. What do we need to do to defeat her?'

'The Dream Witch rules by fear,' Ephemia counselled. 'Destroy that fear and she's done for.'

'But how? Her curses and spells are endless.'

'Aha! You see how she works? The thought of conquering her spells seems impossible. It makes you afraid. Already she has you.'

'No she doesn't. I just want a plan, that's all. It's one thing to be brave. It's another thing to be stupid.'

Ephemia scratched her ear with her hind paw. 'Here it is, then: The Dream Witch makes her potions and spells in her private chambers. They're beneath her forest cottage at the end of her underground labyrinth. We must confront her power at its source.'

Milo's voice came alive with terror and excitement. 'I woke up there with the other stolen children. She took me down some stairs to her study. There were piles of spell books and a writing desk with a stack of parchments made of bat wings.'

'Those spell books are the keys to the visions she makes,' Ephemia declared.

'How do you know?' Olivia asked.

Ephemia puffed up her chest. 'Once upon a time, those spell books were mine. She stole them from me while I was lost in daydreams.'

'Dreams.' Olivia's brow furrowed. 'Tell me this: If the witch's visions aren't real, how can they hurt us?'

'Imagination is a powerful thing,' Ephemia said darkly. 'What we *believe* – what we *think* we know – can destroy us. The creatures and landscapes of the Dream Witch are deadly real within her lair. If you die in her dreams, you die in the real world too.'

Olivia gripped for the pysanka, wrapped in the pocket of her cloak. 'But we have the talisman.'

'Yes. And as long as you keep it safe beside you, she can't come near. But never doubt her cunning. She'll try to use her phantoms to destroy it. So stay alert.'

'No worries there,' Milo said.

'Good,' Ephemia said. 'I'll help as I can. I may not be able to keep my spells straight, but my mousley form has connected me to nature. I've learned how to listen to the world: to speak the languages of fur and feather; to hear the whispers in leaves and vines; and to know the way of lowly things. All this I put to your service.'

Olivia kissed Ephemia on the forehead. 'Thank you.'

The three friends looked past the fields of corn to the forest silhouetted against the starry sky.

Olivia cleared her throat. 'Onward, then, to the witch's cottage.'

And off they went.

A MATTER OF HONOUR

Perspiration oozed from Leo's scalp. It soaked his greasy hair, trickled into his ears, dripped off his chin, and inflamed the glistening pustules on his cheeks and forehead.

'Please, Uncle, I don't want to go.'

The prince was with the duke in the castle stable; fifty cavalry were horsed and waiting outside in the courtyard. The soldier who'd been tossed down the well had been swept into the marsh, where he'd found Olivia and Milo's footprints in the muddy banks. He'd followed them to a ditch along a road leading through the countryside towards the forest. Now all that remained was for the prince to lead his troops in pursuit.

His uncle planted his feet between the manure piles. 'You're heir to the Pretonian throne, boy,' he glowered, meaty hands on meatier hips. 'And you're afraid to take what's yours? That princess is your prize – a prize snatched from under your nose by a peasant. You'd let that stand?'

'N-not usually, no,' Leo stammered. 'But the Dream Witch is about.'

'That didn't frighten the princess. She hopped down a well. Are you telling me a little caged birdie has more courage than a Pretonian prince? What will your father say if he hears you've shamed him?'

'What will he say if he hears I'm dead?'

'He'll boast he had a son who died battling a witch, and order a glorious state funeral, of course. You'll have a parade, monuments, and ceremonial wreaths so grand they'll empty every florist in the kingdom.'

'But I'll be dead!' Leo's armoured knees

knocked together. There was a terrible clang.

The duke pressed his index finger on his nephew's nose. 'Listen to me, boy: You have a responsibility to the honour of the Pretonian throne. Re-capture that girl or earn your father's contempt now and forever.'

'Please, Uncle, no,' Leo sniffled. 'Aside from the witch, I'm afraid I could fall off my horse.'

'Why? Are you an idiot?'

'No. But I can't gallop. The men will laugh at me.'

'They'll laugh even harder if you don't hoist your tail onto your trusty steed and lead them to glory.'

Leo withered under his uncle's scorn. He whimpered over to his horse, a mighty beast with fearsome hooves, a braided mane, and steam shooting from its nostrils. Then he wiped his nose, slithered up a stepladder and crawled onto the saddle.

The duke passed him his helmet; a warrior's envy with a chainmail collar, steel visor, and red plumes. Leo put it on.

'A true Pretonian prince,' his uncle said. 'You look the part. Now act it.'

With that, he smacked the horse's rump. The beast reared up with a whinny and charged into the courtyard, the shrieking prince clinging to its reins.

INTO THE WOODS

The road turned at the last cornfield before the forest. The cornstalks towered above them. Beyond the first row all the friends could see was a jungle of darkness.

'What to do?' Ephemia fretted. 'We can't make a noise; the Evil One may be near. On the roads and in the ditches I could warn you about rocks and potholes. But the corn is so dense I don't know how to guide you without a racket of rustling and crunching.'

'I know how to walk these fields with my eyes closed,' Milo volunteered. 'I used to do it for fun.' He turned to Olivia. 'Put your hand on my shoulder. Keep to my pace. We'll be at the edge of the forest in no time.'

Olivia did as she was told and the pair moved forward, their progress silent save for their breaths. Olivia imagined the ears of corn bending to hear their heartbeats. She pictured messages sent root by root to the Dream Witch in her lair. But that was impossible. Wasn't it?

There was a sudden snapping of dried stalks. Something was moving straight ahead. Something that didn't care if it was heard.

Milo and Olivia froze. So did the creature. Whatever it was, it knew they were there. They could feel its eyes peering at them from the dark.

'It's only a fox,' Ephemia murmured.

At the sound of the voice, the animal tore away, kicking up dirt and husks.

Olivia shivered. If this was what it was like to travel through a cornfield, how would her nerves carry her through the witch's underworld? For the first time in memory, life in a turret didn't seem so bad.

'Forward,' Milo whispered calmly. A few more minutes and they were free of the field.

Olivia had only ever seen the forest from a distance. By daylight, from her turret window, it had looked inviting; a retreat so lush and green she could barely believe it was home to the sorceress. But up close at night, its mighty oaks loomed grim as ghostly sentries, their canopy a shroud to hide dark deeds.

Milo and Olivia edged their way through a strip of grasses and under the forest branches at the tree line. From here there'd be no stars to guide them, all light extinguished by the boughs above.

Ephemia coaxed them into the inky void. 'Fallen branch to the right . . . Weasel den to the left,' she navigated, as they crossed the floor of rotting leaves. At first they made good progress, but soon Milo and Olivia were walking in different directions. Keeping them on track was impossible.

'Which way's ahead?' asked Milo, his arms waving blindly in the dark.

'Where do I go now?' from Olivia.

Ephemia sniffed the air and found an inspiration. 'Wait and see!' She tilted her head back and opened her mouth. Out came a sound so high that neither of the friends could hear it – a sound, indeed, as silent as thought.

At once, speckles of greenish light flickered in the air around them. More glimmered by the second, and more and more, all twinkling in the dark.

Milo's eyes grew large: 'Fireflies!'

'Yes,' Ephemia beamed. 'Forest friends.'

Summoned together for a mighty task, the little creatures flitted in from every corner of the bush. They multiplied beyond number, coating rocks and trunks and fallen branches. As they clustered, shapes emerged – trees and shrubs shimmering in an otherworldly green.

Ephemia opened her mouth again and spoke the silent language of the woods: *Show us the way to the Dream Witch's cottage.*

The fireflies flew up from their resting places and gathered themselves into a glowing ball of light. It floated in the air, then swooped down and rolled itself out above the ground like a glittering carpet.

As Olivia, Milo and Ephemia ventured towards the path, the fireflies made way; they hovered ahead, their light leading the trio safely through thickets, around brambles, and over a great log fallen across a stream. They passed three boulders on their left.

'These boulders . . .' Milo whispered. 'I've been here before. The night the Dream Witch caught me.'

Ephemia nodded gravely. 'We're near her lair.'

The air grew musky, ripe with the damp smell of rot. By the dim glow, Olivia and Milo saw mushrooms in profusion, deep reds and yellows and browns; they nested in the spongy wet of decaying stumps and sprouted like saucers from ancient tree trunks. And now there was a new smell, raw and sickly sweet. It was the smell of death.

The fireflies roiled into the air in terror. Wave upon wave, they vanished into the night. For a moment all was still, and then the friends saw glimmers of firelight filtering through a dense cluster of thorn bushes.

'We've arrived,' Ephemia said. 'Step carefully.'

The three tiptoed stealthily around the thicket, the blanket of rotten leaves swallowing up their footsteps. But as they circled, the firelight circled with them. No matter how far they travelled it was always twinkling from the other side of the thorns. By the third time around, it was clear something was very wrong.

'What's going on?' Olivia asked.

'Stay here. I'll go around by myself,' Ephemia said. 'If I chase the light back to this side of the thicket, hide yourselves in the hollowed log to your right.'

Olivia and Milo laid low as Ephemia scurried round the bushes yet again.

'Did you see it?' she asked on her return.

'No,' Olivia said.

'But you must have. It kept opposite me full circle.'

'Maybe that's what *you* saw,' Olivia said. 'From here the light stayed steady on the other side.'

'I think I've got it,' Milo said. 'The night I got caught, I tried to go home. But everything was turned around, all back to front.'

'Back to front!' Olivia understood at once. 'So while we've each been thinking the cottage is in *front* of us, it may actually be *behind*.'

'Exactly.'

'All right then,' Olivia said. 'At the count of three, let's look over our shoulders. One. Two. Three.'

Olivia, Milo and Ephemia glanced backwards. Sure enough, they were suddenly beyond the thicket. The witch's cottage was barely a hundred feet away.

The cottage looked very much as Olivia remembered it from the drawing. Resting at the far end of a small grove, it was surrounded by a hedge of thighbones capped by a row of skulls. Except, as Olivia now realised, the skulls were lamps, each holding a candle whose ghastly flare shone through empty nostrils and eye sockets, and the vines on the cottage walls were, in fact, dark veins throbbing in the skull-light.

At the centre of the fence was an archway; its sides were made of shoulder blades, its canopy an opened ribcage. From here, a path of knuckles and kneecaps led to the front door. Thatching from the roof hung above the entrance like coarse combed hair. Windows on either side stared out, half-shuttered in sleep. As for the door itself – it was a mouth. Hideous lips framed giant teeth that creaked open and shut, as if the cottage had rusty hinges or, perhaps, was snoring.

'It's alive,' Olivia gasped.

Ephemia put a paw to her lips. 'Shh.'

The friends crept to the fence. They slipped quietly under the archway. But the moment they stepped on the path, the skull-lamps flared.

The cottage roused. Its shutters blinked open. Its door of teeth clamped shut. Smoke billowed from its chimney. A fierce red blazed behind its window-eyes.

Something inside was looking out.

Without thinking, Olivia grabbed the pysanka from her pocket and held it in the air before them.

The light dimmed out behind the windows. The shutters closed. There was a pause. Then, once again, the monstrous mouth dozed open and shut, open and shut.

'It's now or never,' Milo said. He pulled a thighbone from the fence and raced to the entrance. When the mouth opened, he wedged it between the teeth. The bone bent as the mouth tried to close. 'Quickly.'

The trio dived through the opening. No sooner were they inside the cottage than the thighbone shattered. The door snapped shut.

They were stuck in a terrible blackness.

Olivia gagged at the warm stench. 'Is everyone all right?'

'I'm fine,' Milo said.

Ephemia jumped on Olivia's shoulder. 'Me too. But oh dear, oh dear!'

'What is it, Ephemia? What do you see?'

Before the mouse could answer, the floor began to rise and fall. Olivia toppled to her knees. Her hands touched something wet and spongy.

'What kind of carpet is this?'

'It's not a carpet,' Ephemia said, as the floor heaved them to the back of the cottage.

'Then what is it?'

'It's a tongue!'

Olivia screamed, as the cottage swallowed them down its earthen gullet into the witch's underworld.

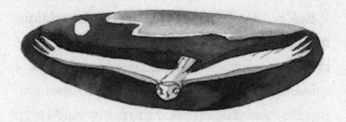

HUNTER AND HUNTED

A nervous rash erupted in Leo's armpits as he led the cavalry out of the castle. The itch was unbearable. Still, it gave him something to think about besides his terror of meeting the witch.

The company rode through the town and down the hill to the marsh, halting at the place where the runaways' tracks had been spotted. The first officer lowered his torch, and peered at the footprints.

'No doubt they thought they were smart to skulk in the ditch,' he said. 'But this mud tells a tale the hard road would have kept secret.'

Leo's Adam's apple bobbled in his throat. 'Where to now?'

'Wherever Your Highness commands.'

Hooray! Then back to the castle, Leo thought. But that was impossible. His men would laugh at him. His voice jumped an octave: 'Follow the footprints.'

The cavalry tracked the trail through the countryside. Leo's rash blossomed. It spread down his sides and into his underpants. He tried to rub his bum against the saddle. The itch got worse.

'There's a camp fire in the valley below,' the first officer said.

They galloped down, but all they found were a man with a wooden foot and a woman huddled by the ashes of a burnt-out homestead. The couple told the soldiers they'd seen no one but a pair of good-hearted children. 'We gave the poor things food and clothing. Are they in trouble?'

'If we find them,' Leo blustered. 'Where did they go?'

Milo's father looked at his wife. 'We don't know.'

'If you're lying, you'll be missing more than a leg,' Leo said.

'Over here,' a soldier called out. He pointed at fresh boot marks.

The trail led to the cornfield by the witch's forest. The tickle in Leo's drawers was unbearable. 'They seem to have vanished,' he said hopefully.

'With respect, Your Highness, I think they went through the corn stalks.'

'Exactly. We've lost them. They could be anywhere in that jungle. If we try to follow them, our torches will burn the field down around us.'

'You'd let them go?'

'No, but I, well . . .'

There was a whoosh in the air above them.

'What was that?' Leo trembled.

The men looked up. A great owl swooped out of the night.

Leo convulsed in terror. His legs flailed, his

arms flapped. The spurs on his feet dug into his horse's flanks. The reins in his hands slapped its neck. The steed charged forward into the cornfield.

'Woah!' Leo cried, bouncing this way and that. But with every bounce he landed a boot with his spurs. The horse galloped faster, out of control.

Leo couldn't think; couldn't breathe. There was corn everywhere. Stalks flayed his face. Cobs boxed his ears. Tassels got up his nose.

His horse burst free of the field. And now – oh no – it hurtled into the forest.

'Stop!' Leo squealed. But the horse paid no heed. Guided by an invisible host, it dodged trees and leapt over brooks, racing at a mad clip, impossible to follow.

How will my men be able to find me? Leo panicked. *What will become of me?*

He grabbed the reins at the bridle and yanked them back sharply. The horse came to a sudden stop. Leo pitched over its head and landed in a raspberry bush.

'Where are you, you mangy beast?' Leo cried. 'Get me out of here.'

The horse grunted as if to say, *Why should I?*

Leo scrambled out of the bush. 'I'll have you sent to the glue factory, just see if I don't. You'll be boiled, deboned, and tossed to the pigs.'

The horse whinnied: *I don't think so.* It turned and trotted merrily into the night.

'Wait. You can't leave me.'

There was a distant neigh, like a laugh. Then silence.

Leo was consumed by dread: *I'm alone in the Dream Witch's forest.* He wasn't sure where to go, but he couldn't stay where he was. He tried to tiptoe. His armour squeaked. Two more steps and he walked into a tree. He turned to his right and tripped over a log.

This is Olivia's fault, Leo wept in fury. *If she hadn't run away, I'd be safe at the castle. Wait till I get my hands on her. I'll teach her who's boss.*

He heard a rustling over his head. Something dived at him out of the dark. A rush of feathers. It flew away.

What was it – that owl again? Maybe. But it was something else, too.

He wasn't alone.

Not ten feet away, he saw two red coals glowing in the dark. Under their glow, he saw a nose like a trunk that disappeared into the pitch black.

'Can I help you?' the stranger said.

Leo's throat went dry as a desert. 'I've l-lost my way. I'd like to get out of these woods.'

'If you'd asked for a basket of toadstools, I'd have obliged. But to escape these woods? Not tonight, I'm afraid.' The eyes floated towards him. He saw the witch's withered frame, her long curled fingernails, and a nose that went on forever. The owl was perched on her right shoulder.

'Dream Witch.'

'Clever boy.'

'What do you want?' Leo panicked. 'My heart?'

The Dream Witch chuckled. 'Do you have one? Ah, but of course you do. It's beating so fast I'm surprised it doesn't pop out of your mouth and run away.'

'P-please. L-let me go. My father, the King of Pretonia, will pay a ransom.'

'Really?'

'Yes,' Leo gulped. 'I think so.'

'You *think* so, but you're not *sure*, are you? I wouldn't be either. Why pay gold to rescue a coward who shames his name, when a son who died on a noble quest would make the family proud?'

Leo shuddered. 'So what are you going to do? Grind me up and eat me?'

The witch's nose inhaled his terror. 'What a splendid idea.'

Leo threw up in his helmet.

'Oh for heaven's sake, there's no need to be disgusting,' the witch chided. 'Can't I have a little fun?' She paused. 'The Princess Olivia and her friend have breeched my underworld. They dare to threaten my power. My spirits will destroy them, but nothing must be left to chance.' She smiled. 'I'd like to offer you a proposition.'

'Anything, Dream Witch.'

'As long as the princess has her pysanka, I can't come near her or her party. Smash the talisman for me and I'll give you more riches than in all your father's treasuries. So much gold he won't care about the missing girl. He'll be proud of you, boy. Yes, and love you, too.'

Leo couldn't believe his good fortune. 'Thank you, Dream Witch. Thank you. I'll shatter the talisman, and get you the princess and her friend.' He kissed her yellow fingernails. 'Take me to them.'

'Your wish is my command,' the witch winked.

Leo blinked. When he opened his eyes, he was standing outside the Cottage of Dreams.

THE DREAM MARSH

Olivia, Milo and Ephemia spilled out of the earthen gullet into the Dream Witch's underworld.

Olivia had imagined she'd find a series of vast caverns with rot dripping from rock walls and roots growing down from above. Yet the witch's lair was something else again – a vast grey emptiness without end or beginning. Even the grey under their feet seemed to disappear into space. Olivia wondered if she was floating, but a tap of her foot found her standing on some kind of invisible floor.

'So this is the witch's dream world,' she marvelled.

'Yes,' Milo nodded. 'It starts in nothingness.'

'Which way should we go?'

'It doesn't matter,' Ephemia said. 'Nowhere is everywhere: Everywhere is nowhere. The dream will lead you.'

Olivia took a step. The greyness under her feet was slick. She grabbed onto Milo for support. The two of them skidded forward and wobbled to a stop.

'It's slippery as ice,' she gasped.

'Cold as ice, too,' Milo said.

'Of course!' Olivia exclaimed. 'We're standing on ice. Ice as grey as the marsh when it freezes in winter.'

A chill swept around them. Their toes went numb. Their breaths misted. With each breath the mist spread in waves, filling the dream-marsh with an icy fog.

Ephemia snuggled at Olivia's neck. 'Move or you'll freeze to death.'

Olivia remembered watching from her turret

as villagers glided across the frozen marsh on wooden skates. How she'd wished to be with them, making pirouettes and figures of eight. She tried to mimic what she'd seen, but when she pushed forward, her feet slipped out from under her.

Milo reached down and gave her a hand. Olivia tried to pull herself up but toppled him over instead.

'Sorry.'

'Not to worry,' Milo said. 'Roll onto your knees, plant a foot, then push up with your hands.'

He tried to show her how – he'd done it a million times – but *this* time, he couldn't find his balance. He tumbled back down. He tried again. And again and again. Olivia too. No use. Each time, they ended up smack on their backs.

Olivia's teeth chattered. 'What do we do?'

'Crawl,' Ephemia ordered.

They inched forward on hands and knees: their fingers white with cold; their nails blue. A wind whipped up against them. Pellets of icy mist stung their cheeks. They slid backwards.

Through the gusts, Olivia heard the voice of a little girl: *Help me.*

'I hear a child,' Olivia hollered over the wind.

'You're imagining things,' Milo hollered back. 'The children are in the witch's lair.'

'No. There's one nearby. Maybe she escaped.'

Help me. Help me.

The voice was coming from below. Olivia looked down. The ice was covered with sleet. She rubbed it clear.

Through wisps of fog, a little girl's face stared up at her from under the frozen sheet; her head was in a pocket of air where the ice was thin. The child was near death, her skin a bluish-grey, her long hair spread out in the frigid water. She scratched at the surface from below: *Help me.*

'She's here, under the ice,' Olivia shouted. 'We have to break it. We have to save her.'

'No,' Ephemia shrieked.

'What do you mean, no?' Olivia whirled her head to Milo. 'Milo, help me!'

But Milo's eyes were wide with terror. He

pointed towards the child. Olivia looked back and saw what her friends saw: The little girl's fingers weren't fingers. They were claws. Claws attached to tentacles with suckers the size of plates.

Olivia screamed.

The beast threw off its disguise. Its little-girl mouth stretched wide, as it rolled its lips over its forehead and down past its shoulders, revealing a brain sack with a single bulbous eye and a fierce beak. The tentacles swirled in the gelid water as the creature beat and clawed at the underside of the ice.

The surface cracked.

'Ephemia, save us!' Olivia cried. 'Cast a spell!'

'I'll only make things worse.'

'They *can't* get worse!'

True, Ephemia thought. For the first time since Olivia's birth, she rummaged her memory for a spell: '*Amnibitor Imnabatar Praxit!*'

And things got worse. The brain sack ballooned. The tentacles swelled. A rubbery limb broke through and shot high in the air. It slapped down by Olivia's head, splitting the surface of the ice.

Ephemia tried to fix things. *'Omnobiter Nimtarbiter Traxip!'*

And worse. The creature multiplied into three beasts, each larger than the first. Their tentacles smashed the ice field into chunks. Olivia and Milo found themselves on a slab that bobbed in the swells as the creatures thrashed below. All around, massive cubes of ice upended. Wedges splintered and cast adrift.

The largest creature wrapped a tentacle around a corner of their slab, and pulled down with its suckers. The ice-raft tilted. Milo and Olivia grabbed the upper edge. The monster raised its head. Olivia lost her grip. She slid towards its open beak.

'Nimnobiter Traxibiter Bixit!' Ephemia squealed.

A giant umbrella, twenty-feet long, shot down through the fog. Its shaft speared the creature's eye. With a howl, the beast ripped out the missile, flung it across the pitching slab, and plunged back into the marsh.

'A parasol? Really?' Olivia demanded.

'With my luck it could have been a feather. Be happy you're alive.'

'But not for long,' Milo exclaimed.

On either side, the remaining beasts emerged from the mists. Their tentacles swept the ice in search of their prey.

'I've got it! The parasol!' Olivia shouted. 'Ephemia, you're a genius after all.'

Quickly, she and Milo cupped themselves inside the giant handle and undid the mighty clasp.

A snippet of wind caught the inside of the umbrella. The fabric ballooned open; its broad canopy was like a giant sail. It propelled them across the marsh. Holding on for dear life, Olivia and Milo's heels skimmed over the water, skipping from one ice chunk to the next.

The creatures gave chase, their tentacles flying through the air.

Dead ahead, a barge of ice bobbed up from below.

'We're going to crash!' Olivia cried, as rubbery limbs slapped at their heels.

'No we're not,' Milo exclaimed, 'Jump!'

They leapt together, bouncing onto the wedge. In a blink, they skied up and over the top. For a moment, they swayed, suspended in the air, the umbrella a giant parachute.

Slimy suckers flew through the fog around them. The end of a tentacle whipped around Olivia's left boot. The creature tightened its grip. The umbrella careened in the wind.

'It's got me,' Olivia said. 'Ephemia, Milo, save yourselves. I'm letting go.'

'No, don't give up,' Milo shouted. 'That's what the Dream Witch wants you to do.' He shinnied up the handle. 'Grab my leg.'

Olivia clutched Milo's knee. He shimmied higher, pulling her with him. The creature's grip held tight to the leather boot. But Olivia's foot slipped up the inside. She kicked it free.

Released from the creature's pull, the umbrella shot high in the air current. Soon the friends were sailing far above the fog. By the time it cleared, they were ages from the marsh.

The wind calmed to a gentle breeze. The umbrella floated down. Stretching to the horizon, Olivia, Milo and Ephemia saw gardens lusher than any courtyard with flowers high as houses.

'It looks like heaven,' Olivia marvelled.

'A heaven made in hell,' Ephemia murmured darkly.

The umbrella landed on top of a peony bush the size of an oak tree. Olivia and Milo climbed down its mighty branches.

'So there you are!' came a voice from a patch of bluebells. Olivia whirled around. A sword scythed through the thicket of stems. A young man stepped forward. 'I've come to save you.'

Oh no, Olivia thought.

It was Leo.

AN UNEXPECTED ENCOUNTER

Olivia looked Leo in the eye. 'I don't need saving, and certainly not by the likes of you.'

'In fact, she needs saving *from* you,' said Ephemia.

Leo's eyes bulged. 'It talks.'

The spunky mouse puffed up her chest. '*It* has a name and the name is Ephemia. I can do more than talk, too, in case you've forgotten.'

Leo raised a boot. 'Another word and I'll squish you.'

Milo picked up a pebble the size of a rock. 'Stay where you are.'

'Who are you to tell me what to do?'

'The best aim in the county. Take another step and I'll bop you.'

'So you're Olivia's knight in not-so-shiny armour, are you?' Leo sneered. 'Little Sir Corn Cob?'

'He's a friend,' Olivia said. 'Treat him with respect.'

'Oh, of course,' Leo mocked. 'How else to treat a peasant who broke into your chamber to steal you for the Dream Witch?' He looked back at Milo. 'How much is the witch paying you to betray the princess? What's your reward?'

'We might ask the same of you,' Ephemia declared.

'I'm a prince,' Leo said. 'I get what I want and always will. I don't need rewards.'

'How many others came with you?' Milo demanded. 'Where are they?'

'It's none of your business, but I came alone.'

'You? Alone?' Olivia frowned. 'That's hard to believe.'

'How dare you question my valour? I'm Crown Prince of Pretonia!'

'Yes, and you run from castle ghosts,' Ephemia laughed. She put on her phantom voice, ''Tis I, Weaselkins, the Headless Hunchback of Horning!'

'That was you?' Leo flashed his sword.

Milo gripped his rock.

'Enough,' Olivia exclaimed. 'This is no time to fight. The witch's world can turn upside down in a second. So – both of you – put down your weapons. Now.'

The boys looked from Olivia to each other and back again. Then, wary as foxes, they disarmed.

'Now, Leo, the truth,' Olivia said. 'Where are your troops?'

'Back at the castle probably,' Leo said. 'I led some cavalry into the forest. But when we reached the witch's cottage, we were attacked by demons. My men abandoned me. I hid behind the door of teeth.'

'And got swallowed into this underworld,' Olivia said.

'Yes,' Leo nodded. 'I've no idea where I've

been or how I got here. Things came at me out of nowhere. Then I heard your voices. And here I am.'

'So, you *are* a liar. You didn't show up to save the princess,' Milo scoffed.

Leo hung his head. He hoped it passed for shame, for he realised that if he was going to destroy Olivia's pysanka he had to gain their trust. And there's nothing like truth with a dash of guile to grease the wheels of treachery.

'It's true,' Leo choked. 'I'm no hero. I'm a coward. A bully. A miserable failure.' With great effort, he squeezed out a tear.

Olivia's heart melted on cue. 'Please don't cry.'

'Why not?' Leo helped himself to a sniffle and sank onto a giant mushroom cap. 'I was raised to be King of Pretonia: A warrior, hard and cruel. Well, now I have my reward. I'm alone, without a friend in the world. I don't deserve any. In fact, I don't deserve to live. Ask anyone. Even my father.' He broke into sobs. To his surprise, some of them were real.

Milo turned away in embarrassment.

Ephemia wiped her eyes with her tail. 'You poor, poor boy.'

Olivia ran and knelt by the prince; his stink was overwhelming, but it wasn't the time to be unkind. 'We didn't get off to a good start,' she said. 'But I know what it's like to feel trapped in a life that isn't your own.'

'You understand?'

Olivia struggled to find the right words. 'Deep inside, I know you can't be nearly as horrible as you seem.'

'Thank you,' Leo wept. 'So, you forgive me?'

'What else *can* I do?'

Leo kissed her hand.

Olivia wiped it on the back of her coat and turned to Ephemia and Milo. 'What do you say? Prince Leo needs our help and can help us in return. Can we let bygones be bygones?'

'Of course,' Ephemia said. 'As long as we keep our eyes open.'

'Milo?'

Milo wanted to spit. Instead, he shrugged.

'Sure. Why not? He's got a sword at least.'

'Good,' Olivia said. So now –'

But before she could ask which way they should go, the company heard a delicate whirr in the air over by a stand of tulips. Then silence.

'What was it?' she whispered. 'What *is* it?'

Leo frowned. 'There's nothing there but those flowers.'

'But I heard something.'

'So did I,' Ephemia said.

Olivia squinted hard, but whatever it was seemed invisible.

Milo glanced at Leo. 'Shall we take a look?'

Leo shook his head so fast it nearly flew off his shoulders. 'If there's something there, we should leave it alone.'

'Whatever it is, it's watching us,' Olivia said. 'I can feel it.'

'I feel it too,' Milo nodded. He took a step towards the tulips. 'Who's there?'

Whatever it was stayed still.

'You three stay here,' Milo said. 'I'm going to investigate.'

'Let me,' Ephemia offered. 'I'm smaller.'

Milo shook his head. 'You need to protect Olivia.'

'Oh really? I'm not a baby,' Olivia shot back. 'If there's danger, I need to take my share.'

'There's enough danger here for all of us,' Milo said. 'This one's on me.'

'Yes, this one's on him,' Leo agreed, and dived under the mushroom cap.

'So much for brave Pretonian princes,' Ephemia muttered.

Milo picked up his rock and approached the giant tulips. Thick, green leaves thrust out of the ground, rising halfway up the mighty stalks before collapsing backwards under their own weight. Dewdrops the size of bowling balls clung to their surface. Towering above the leaves, massive cups of red petals perched at the tips of the stalks, every tip a perfect lookout.

Milo peered up at the flower heads, searching for a sign of the unseen presence. Nothing: every petal was perfectly in place. His neck prickled. Whatever was spying on him wasn't watching from above. It was over by a leaf to his right.

Two droplets on the leaf caught his eye. At a glance, they looked like all the others, each as big as his head. But instead of being clear, they were a pale green.

Milo realised, to his horror, that the droplets weren't droplets at all. They were eyes on a monstrous green head, camouflaged against the leaf. Milo stared as the creature's hideous shape emerged. Now he could see the long green body. The grisly mandibles. The spiked forelegs raised as if in prayer.

Milo struggled to stay calm. 'It's a giant praying mantis.'

PREY

The mantis flickered its papery wings.

'Stay absolutely still,' Ephemia warned. 'If you move it'll strike.'

'Talk to it,' Olivia whispered urgently. 'Make it leave us alone.'

'I can't,' Ephemia said, eyes riveted on the mantis. 'Meat-eaters don't listen when they're hungry.'

'Leo,' Olivia begged. 'Help us.'

Leo shrank behind the fungal stem. 'How?'

'Wave your sword.'

'And draw attention? Are you crazy?'

'Then give your sword to me.'

'No.'

'Fine, be that way,' Olivia said. She slipped off her cloak, and held it in front of her. 'Milo, I'm going to make a distraction. When I say Go—'

Too late. The mantis pounced. Milo was hurled to the ground. He smashed the rock on the insect's mandibles. It reared in fury.

Olivia roared forward waving her cloak. The mantis twisted its head to the flapping cloth. It flew to attack the intruder. Olivia unfurled her cloak to protect herself. The mantis caught it in its claws and tossed it towards a jungle of weeds. A flash of silver fell from the pocket.

'The pysanka!' Ephemia cried, as the mantis toppled Olivia. It held her fast, one foreleg on her chest, the other on her stomach.

Milo jumped on its back and pounded its steely thorax. The mantis ignored him and prepared to chew off Olivia's head.

At that moment, something huge jumped under the boughs of the peony bush. A long red carpet shot through the air and lashed around the mantis' abdomen. In a flash, the force threw

Milo off the insect's thorax and tore Olivia from its grasp. The mantis snapped back under the bush.

'What was that?' Olivia gasped.

The visitor leapt forward. It was the biggest frog she'd ever seen. Bits of the mantis clung to its rubbery lips. Its glassy eyes extended out of their sockets and shoved the leftovers down its throat. Then it blinked blankly, gave a satisfied croak, and hopped away.

Leo scrambled out from under the mushroom. 'Well done,' he said. 'I guess we showed that mantis who was boss.'

Ephemia ignored him. 'Olivia, your pysanka. When the mantis tossed your cloak, it fell out of your pocket. I saw the silver case.'

Leo pricked up his ears. 'Where did it land?'

'In those weeds, by the grove of dandelions.'

If ever there was a time to destroy Olivia's talisman, this was it, and Leo knew it. He imagined the Dream Witch's treasures pouring down around him; heard the cheers of the court; saw the pride in his father's eyes. *I'll never be mocked again,* he thought. *The world will do as I say.*

Leo ran to the giant weeds and swung his sword at a sprawl of crabgrass. Olivia and Milo scrambled in his wake. Together they dodged the toppling purple seed heads, pausing only for Leo to sneeze and itch.

Ephemia suffered no such delay. She zipped over and under the jungle of stems. The dandelions were just beyond the next rock.

'Over here,' the mouse squeaked. She leapt on the stone. 'Oh no.'

Leo, Olivia and Milo carved through the undergrowth.

'What is it?' Olivia demanded.

'There, where your pysanka landed . . .' Ephemia pointed to a hole, six-feet wide, that descended deep into the ground. A few feet below the surface, thick dandelion taproots broke through the earthen side and dangled like vines into the subterranean dark.

Olivia ran to the opening. 'How are we to get the pysanka out of this hole?'

'Stay back,' Ephemia cried. 'It isn't an ordinary hole.'

'What is it then?

'A mole's burrow.'

Olivia leapt back. 'But moles are tiny,' she gasped.

'Not in this world.'

DOWN THE BURROW

Olivia's palms went moist; her flesh crawled. She'd first seen a mole when she was three, playing in the castle garden with the servants' children. The mole had poked its little head out of a hole in the grass and quickly disappeared. Olivia had laughed at the sight of its furry snout, teeny red eyes, and clownish paws.

The royal gardener, a rough-hewn stump of a man, hadn't been so amused; he'd cursed the pest who'd potted his carefully tended lawn, and thrust his spade into the earth. Olivia's heart filled with pity that the creature might have been killed, but her pity soon turned to terror. The gardener had unearthed the vermin's pantry, a tiny cave it had hollowed out and filled with worms and beetles. They all looked dead, but the gardener knew better.

'These poor things fell into Mr Mole's burrows. He freezed 'em with a poison in his spit. Then he dragged 'em to his larders to feed on at his pleasure. That's right, little Princess, he eats 'em alive. Slowly. Bit by bit.'

Olivia pictured a giant mole. *What if it does that to us?* she wondered.

'Milo and I can take care of this,' Leo said gallantly.

Milo gave him a funny look. 'You want to brave danger?'

'Indeed,' Leo said slyly. 'I need to prove myself worthy of your company.'

'There's hope for you yet,' Ephemia exclaimed.

'But *I* should go,' Olivia insisted. 'It's my pysanka.'

'No. You helped with the mantis. Me, I need to redeem myself,' Leo said.

'He's right,' Ephemia agreed. 'You mustn't deny him. It would be cruel. You and I can help from above. We'll hide under that dandelion leaf and guard the burrow entrance, in case some creature comes sniffing.'

'Please?' Leo wheedled. He put on his best pleading face, the one he used to lure milk-maids close enough for a pinch.

'All right,' Olivia said. 'But if there's trouble, I'll be there.'

Leo and Milo lowered their legs down the burrow. Each grabbed a taproot, tested his weight, and began the descent, as if rappelling down a rope.

Milo was faster. In fact, he was soon so much further down that he wondered if Leo had returned to the surface. He looked up and saw Leo's feet. The prince kicked the side of the burrow. Loose dirt fell into Milo's face. He coughed, swinging blindly on the vine.

'You idiot,' he exclaimed, wiping his eyes

with a forearm. 'I could have broken my neck.'

'Sorry,' Leo lied. 'I've never climbed down a mole hole before.' His breath caught in his throat. 'Look. Do you see that sparkle?'

Milo squinted. Not twelve feet below, the silver sheath of the pysanka lay glinting on the ground. His heart pounded with excitement and fear. 'We've reached the floor of the burrow. I can see tunnels opening in three directions.'

A low, snuffling sound echoed out of the dark. Milo held his breath. He heard steps, padding up the tunnel, and the sucking of lips and spit, the chitter of teeth.

He tried to scramble up the root. 'Quick, Leo! The mole! It's coming!'

'Not for me,' Leo smiled and sliced Milo's vine with his sword.

Milo tumbled to the ground. 'What are you doing?'

'Why, waiting for the mole to carry you away, stupid. There's only room for one hero in this story. You, my friend, are an accident paving my way to glory.'

The vermin pounced. It clutched Milo in its scaly paws.

Milo saw its snout. He smelled its breath. He fainted.

Leo watched the mole drag Milo away to its larder. Then he slid down and grabbed the pysanka. He wanted to pry open the silver case and smash the egg then and there. But what if other moles were lurking? Why risk becoming a vermin's lunch?

Leo slipped the talisman inside his breast-plate and shimmied up the vine, determined to smash the egg when he was out of the burrow and alone. As he neared the surface, he planned a simple story.

'Help!' he shrieked as he climbed over the lip of the burrow. 'Help!'

Olivia and Ephemia ran out from under the dandelion leaf.

'What's the matter?' Olivia cried. 'Where's Milo?'

'Milo! Poor Milo!' Leo wailed. 'The mole! It was terrible!'

Olivia grabbed him by the shoulders. 'What happened?'

Leo howled piteously. Olivia slapped his face to bring him to his senses. Leo almost slapped her back, but remembered he was supposed to be in shock.

'W-we reached the bottom of the hole,' he stammered. 'The p-pysanka was nowhere to be seen. We searched down one of the tunnels. The m-mole surprised us. It grabbed Milo in its claws.'

Olivia clutched her chest. 'Oh no.'

'Oh, yes, Princess. Milo is dead. I saw him in the vermin's grip. I saw it drag him off to its larder.'

Without thinking, Olivia dropped to the ground and swung her legs over the hole.

'What are you doing?' Ephemia gaped.

'Going for Milo, what do you think?'

Leo blinked. 'But he's dead.'

'You don't know that. You only saw him carried away. Maybe I can save him.'

'From the mole's larder?' Ephemia gasped.

'You'll only get *yourself* killed as well.'

Leo's mind raced; the witch would not be amused if Olivia's heart was eaten by a mole. 'Your mouse is right,' he said. 'Would Milo want you risking your life for him? Think of your friend – and those children trapped in the witch's spice grinders. You need to stay alive to rescue them. Don't be selfish.'

'I can't help it,' Olivia said. 'I can't leave my friend to be eaten alive. I just *can't!*'

'Then let me go in your place,' Ephemia pleaded.

'No. People have gone in my place too often already. Besides, I'd be left alone with *that* one.' She glanced at the prince. 'Sorry, Leo, but I don't exactly trust you.' She grabbed a tap root. 'Wish me luck.'

Ephemia raised a paw. 'Olivia—'

But the princess was already sliding down the root-vine.

THE MOLE'S LARDER

Olivia lowered herself to the ground, careful lest the tiniest sound alert the mole. The air was thick with the smell of damp fur. At least there was no smell of blood; good – that meant Milo hadn't been ripped to pieces.

Olivia looked around. Tunnels ran off in three directions, each dimly lit by shafts of distant light filtering down from holes burrowed to the surface. Paw prints ran in all directions.

Which way to go? Olivia wondered.

Her heart skipped a beat: Two furrows in the loose soil disappeared up the darkest tunnel. Milo's heels dragging behind the mole?

Olivia rubbed her arms and legs with earth to dull her scent from the mole's inquisitive nose. Then she edged up the trail on tiptoes, barely daring to breathe. The farther she went, the staler the air became.

The walls of the tunnel widened. A small spill of light from a surface hole on the far side revealed a shadowy place filled with a hill of dark, glistening shapes. Olivia reached out to touch them. Her right hand pressed into thick rolls of cold, slimy flesh. She yanked her hand back in horror. Earthworms. She'd touched a mountain of giant earthworms, all of them waiting to be eaten by the mole. Why – she was in the mole's pantry!

From the other side of the cavern, she heard a chittering sound. The mole had arrived from the far tunnel. What could she do? Where could she go?

An arm reached out of the sickening heap, grabbed her, and pulled her into the pile. Olivia slid between the gooey rolls, her hair and skin slick with their ooze. She tried to scream, but her mouth filled with worm.

'Shh,' a voice whispered.

Olivia spat and covered her lips. 'Milo?'

Milo gave her arm a reassuring squeeze. 'Yes,' he murmured. 'The mole grabbed me and I fainted. It must have thought I was dead or it would've paralysed me. I woke up on top of this worm-hill, and swam down to hide among their bodies.'

Milo's grip tightened. They could hear the mole beyond the wall of food.

The creature shrieked in fury at the disappearance of its most recent catch. It sniffed the air. The fetid sweetness of the worms filled its senses. But another aroma mingled in the stink – disguised, perhaps, but there all the same: the smell of human.

The mole let loose a guttural trill: Its treat hadn't escaped. It was hiding. But where? It churned the earth with its massive paws. No luck. It turned to the mountain of worms.

There was a terrible squishing sound as the mole crawled over its paralysed captives. Milo and Olivia felt the pressure as the worms pressed down over their heads. They sank under the weight, and squirmed as nubby ends tickled down their shirts.

The mole prowled forward. The rubbery torsos rolled and twisted with each step.

Milo took Olivia's hand. 'Follow me.'

Together, they trailed below the mole's wake, taking cover in the undulations of the worms. The mucky slime greased their slide through the fleshy jungle.

'We should be nearing the tunnel at the far side of the pantry,' Milo murmured. 'Before I dived into the mound, I saw a shaft of light at the entrance. If we can make it there, we can try and escape.'

The mole stopped in its tracks. There was nothing on top of its food stores. That meant only one thing: Its prey was beneath.

The mole thrust itself down into the pile. Olivia and Milo moved out of its way. They bumped into a beetle. Using its shell as both shield and disguise, they slogged their way out of the heap. It was like wading through rooms of clammy noodles.

'There! The light, the roots,' Milo pointed excitedly as they broke through. They raced for the exit, and began their ascent before the mole had time to realise they were gone. Olivia had never thought of herself as a climber. Now, picturing herself as a feast for the beast, she knew she could scale the tunnel in an instant.

They neared the surface.

'I have to warn you about Leo,' Milo grunted as he climbed. 'He tried to kill me. He cut the root I was climbing and left me for the mole.'

'What?'

'He's a traitor. I'll bet in league with the Dream Witch.'

'Ephemia,' Olivia gulped. 'I left her with him. She's in danger.' The princess climbed faster.

'Yes,' Milo said, scrambling after. 'And another thing. Leo and I found the pysanka. It was at the base of the burrow.'

'He must have it, then. It wasn't there when I climbed down.'

'We have to get it back or he'll smash it.'

'If he hasn't already.'

Olivia pulled herself up onto level ground. Milo followed right after. In the distance, they spotted the dandelions that towered above the hole they'd climbed down and ran towards them. But when they got there, there was no sign of Ephemia or Leo.

'Maybe they're hiding,' Milo said.

'It's only us,' Olivia called out.

Silence.

Olivia touched her hand to her heart. 'They're gone.'

A PARTING OF THE WAYS

'They *can't* be gone,' Milo exclaimed. 'Where would they go?'

Olivia looked around in desperation. 'Ephemia?'

A shadow crossed their heads. Olivia and Milo looked up. The Dream Witch's owl circled above with a mouse in its talons.

'Ephemia!' Olivia screamed.

The owl hooted, as if laughing at some cruel joke, and flew away.

'Ephemia!!!'

Olivia's head swam. She collapsed onto

Milo's shoulder. 'This is my fault. How could I have left her?'

Milo had no idea what to say or do. He'd never been held by a girl before, much less one who was crying. 'It's all right,' he comforted.

'What do you mean it's all right,' Olivia wept.

'I mean it's *not* all right. Of course it's not. But maybe it's not what it seems.'

'It *is*,' Olivia wept. 'You *know* it.'

'I do, yes, you're right, I know,' Milo babbled. 'But Leo—'

'Ephemia's gone! How can you think about Leo?'

'I can't. I don't. I haven't.'

'Then why did you say his name?' Olivia pounded his shoulder in frustration.

'Olivia, ow, listen,' Milo said. 'There's nothing we can do about Ephemia. But Leo – he has the pysanka. It's all that stands between you and the witch. Ephemia fought for your life. You have to fight too.'

Olivia wiped the tears from her eyes. Her

voice quivered: 'You're right. We need to find Leo. We can't let the Dream Witch win.'

On cue, there were a series of distant wails.

'Leo?'

Olivia and Milo ran towards the sounds. They found a path with Leo's boot prints and hurried along it. The wails turned into shrieks. 'Help! Save me!'

They burst into a clearing by a patch of daffodils. Leo was stuck on a web strung between two flowers. A spider was binding him like a mummy. The pair jumped backwards, but the insect was too busy with its prey to pay them heed.

'Save me,' Leo pleaded.

'Why should we?' Olivia said. 'You called the witch's owl to snatch Ephemia.'

'I didn't. I ran when the owl swooped down and got stuck in this web. I don't know what happened to your mouse.'

The spider knit its web around his head.

'AAAH! HELP ME!'

'First, why did you leave me for the mole?' Milo demanded.

'And what did you do to my pysanka?' Olivia chimed in.

'I don't know what you're talking about,' Leo squealed as the spider's legs brushed against his cheeks.

'I'll bet you don't,' Olivia said. She and Milo turned on their heels.

'No, wait, I'll tell you!' Leo screeched. The spider gagged him. 'MMMMM! MMMMM!'

Olivia and Milo looked at each other and nodded.

'All right then,' Olivia said. 'We'll spare you. But you don't deserve it.'

The prince's sword had fallen at his feet. Milo grabbed it, and swung it at the spider's head. The insect reared on its hind legs. Milo sliced the strands on the left of Leo's cocoon. The frayed web blew in the breeze, as the spider retreated behind a flower.

Milo cut the strands on the right. Leo fell to the ground, tangled in his bindings.

'I'll cut you free if you tell us what happened to the pysanka,' Milo said.

'It's inside my breastplate.'

'You said you couldn't find it.'

'I was confused.'

'You were lying!'

Milo carved the cocoon from around Leo, then wrapped his hands in leaves to pull away the final sticky bits. He retrieved the pysanka and gave it to Olivia.

'How can I ever repay you?' Leo grovelled.

'You can't,' Olivia said coldly. She hung the talisman around her neck and beneath her shirt by its little gold chain. 'Make your way back to the castle. Tell your uncle to leave Bellumen by dawn or he'll have me to deal with.'

'You?'

'Yes, me.' Olivia looked him in the eye. 'I'm not the little girl you met this afternoon. Then I knew my title, but not who I am inside, nor what I can do or be. I've found out so many things since then. And one of the most important things I've found out is that I've bigger things to be afraid of than you and your uncle.'

'Nice speech,' Leo laughed.

'Let's see if you laugh now you're on your own,' Milo glared.

'On my own? You're joking.'

'Not on your life,' Olivia said. 'We offered you friendship and you betrayed us.'

'How will I survive?' Leo quaked.

'You have a sword,' said Milo, throwing the weapon at his feet. 'That's more than we have.'

'Besides,' Olivia added, 'your friend the Dream Witch will protect you.'

'She's not my friend.'

Olivia raised an eyebrow. 'Goodbye, Leo.' She turned to go.

'Wait, you *can't* leave,' Leo blustered. 'I forbid it. I'm Leo, Crown Prince of Pretonia!'

'Well, I'm Olivia, Crown Princess of I-Don't-Care.'

With that, she and Milo marched into the unknown.

'You'll pay for this,' Leo snarled under his breath. 'Just wait and see.'

HAIR, NAIL, AND GRINDINGS

Back at the castle, Leo's uncle was having a fitful sleep. He'd taken the bedroom next to Olivia's parents, but even its rich velvet canopies and goose down pillows had failed to ease his mind.

After sending off his nephew to capture the princess, the duke had had uneasy thoughts. Chasing down an unarmed girl and a peasant boy shouldn't be a problem, especially when accompanied by fifty armed cavalry. But Leo was a special case: if there were a way to mess things up, the idiot would find it. Then what? Despite the duke's bluster about heroic deaths, he knew that Leo's father would be none too pleased if his heir came to harm.

So the duke tossed and turned, his dreams made worse by indigestion. His bum trumpet ripped the air; the gases billowed the bed sheets. With each foul blast, he heard a cannon's roar and pictured Leo leading a charge into a sulphurous bog.

The duke leapt from his bed, still fast asleep, and tried to follow the brat. Ahead, he saw two red coals glowing in the mist: The eyes of the Dream Witch.

Come after me if you dare, the apparition cackled.

'If I dare?' the duke exclaimed. 'I fear no she-devil!'

Imagining himself in full battle gear, he sleepwalked down the castle corridors, swinging his arm as if brandishing a sword. Sentries cleared a path; they knew better than to wake their master when he was in a state.

The apparition descended a rocky cliff – the castle's spiral staircase.

The duke followed. 'Yes, run from me, witch!'

They crossed a plain of pebbles – the cobble-stoned courtyard – and entered a cave.

'I have you now,' the duke bellowed.

Silly man.

'Silly. Do I look silly?' the duke raged. 'I'll show you who's silly!' He sliced the air with his broadsword. The exertion released an explosion of rump gas so vile it nearly blew a hole in his nightshirt.

The duke blinked awake. He wasn't in a cave; he was in the castle stables. Nor was he in battle gear heaving a sword; he was in his nightshirt, waving a candlestick.

'Good evening,' the Dream Witch purred. Her eyes glowed from a nearby stall.

The duke retreated a step. A great flap of wings descended from the rafters. Owl claws clipped his forehead. The duke turned to run, but something thrust itself out of the dark and wrapped around his neck: It was the witch's nose.

The duke tried to break free, but her trunk

tightened; it pulled him towards her and dropped him, limp, at her feet. The heat of the witch's eyes burned his cheeks. He trembled with fear.

'Why, you're shaking,' the Dream Witch teased. 'But surely you can't be cold. You're hairy as a sheep.' She flicked the air with her tongue. 'Ah, the taste of fear. You're not so very different from your nephew, are you?'

'What have you done with him?'

'Who says I even have him?'

'It's why you're here, isn't it?'

'Well, yes, come to think of it.' The Dream Witch winked. 'He's a waste of air. Your Pretonian heir. Even breaking an egg is too much for him. Still, I need payment for the trouble of keeping him alive.'

'What can I give that you can't conjure?'

'The means to make a living image of the king and queen. Spirits can be conjured to play the role of servants. But poppet parents require greater craft: It's a rare child that cannot tell its own.'

'What must I do?'

'Bring me a hair from the queen's head, and a fingernail from the king.'

The duke frowned. 'Why not enter the castle and take them yourself?'

'I may be a sorceress, but I'm not a thief,' the Dream Witch said. 'I take only what people give me: their deepest hopes and fears; their promises; oh, yes, and their children, who trade their futures for my treasure. From these, I weave my spells, my dreams and nightmares.' She paused. 'A hair from the queen's head, and a fingernail from the king. Have we a deal?'

*

Within minutes, the spice jars rattled as the door to the Dream Witch's cavern creaked open.

'I'm home,' the witch sang merrily. 'Can you guess what I want?'

The terrified children buried their heads between their knees and pressed their backs against their glass cells.

'Oh, come on, guess,' the witch twinkled. 'No need to be shy.'

One little boy was overcome by the shakes. His bottle toppled over.

'Why, hello there.' The Dream Witch unspooled her nose from around her waist and plucked up the jar. 'I smell a boy with salty tears and dirty fingernails.' She curled the jar in front of her face. 'So tell me, precious, what do I want?'

The moppet shrank back. 'Grindings?'

'Clever boy. And why do I want them?'

'To make a spell?'

'Excellent child. A lad like you is far too bright to sit on a shelf with dunderheads. You must come to my study: today's spell needs special spice.'

'I'm not special at all! Really!' the boy begged.

'No need to be modest,' the Dream Witch cackled, and whisked him down the long coal stairs to her study of horrors. The lad shuddered at the sight of the living portrait of the witch at the end of the cavern; the nightmarish murals lining the side walls; and the oak-stump desk the size of a village square with its bonfire candle, sheaf of bats'-wing parchments, and inkwell smelling of death.

The Dream Witch put the boy's bottle to one side. Then she smoothed out her handkerchief with her long, yellow fingernails, while her monstrous trunk rooted about in her pocket.

The nose retrieved its prize – a velvet pouch delivered by the duke from the bedroom of Olivia's parents – and shook it out over the handkerchief. A hair from the queen's head floated down onto the left side of the cloth; the bloodied nail from the king's left thumb fell to its right.

'And now for some special spice,' the Dream Witch said. 'The spice of life.' She picked up the glass jar.

'Why me?' the boy cried.

'I have to use someone, don't I? The king and queen promised me a gift and they didn't keep their promise. I need a spell to put things right.'

198

'But I'm not the one who cheated you!'

'Maybe not. But innocents always pay the price.'

'I don't understand.'

'You will, my child. All it takes is growing up.' She gripped the grinding handle.

'No!' the boy screamed

'Hush,' the Dream Witch cooed. 'This won't hurt much. Well, not for long, anyway.'

The boy wailed uncontrollably.

The Dream Witch wrapped her nose around her temples. 'It's been a long day, my pet, and I have a splitting headache. Any more crankiness and I shall grind and grind until there's nothing left to grind but your eyebrows.'

The boy cowered in silence, as the sorceress turned the handle three times. Slivers of skin and a drizzle of red fell on the queen's hair. The witch put down the bottle and snapped her fingers. A musty spell book flew from the top of a stack and opened itself above her outstretched hand.

'Ah, here we are,' the witch said, turning a

page with the flare of a nostril. '*Somnambulo mortitious vivant.*'

The candle flared and suddenly the tip of the hair from the queen's head rose up from the handkerchief. The witch sang a song in languages long forgotten, commanding the hair like a snake charmer. It coiled and rose and coiled again, the slivers of skin rising around it. The hair became two, then three, multiplying to infinity, as it grew into sinews and muscles and limbs. The skin enveloped the hair-flesh until they moved as one, undulating like dancers in a tango.

The Dream Witch glanced at her spell book. '*Visatato tremulo regianet.*'

Invisible fingers kneaded the tissues like dough. In no time, they were sculpted into the image of Olivia's mother: the eyes a deep blue; the hair a soft brown; the smile aglow. The Dream Witch waved her hand; the thing was instantly clothed in the queen's favourite skirt and bodice, a red brocade embroidered with gold thread, and adorned with a perfect imitation of her finest jewels. A whistle of air through the witch's teeth and it began to breathe.

'Good evening, Queen Sophie,' the Dream Witch said.

The spell-queen blinked. 'Good evening, Milady.'

'Are you set to do my bidding?'

'Your wish is my command.'

'Wait but a minute,' the Dream Witch smiled, 'and I shall conjure you a spell-king.' The sorceress lifted the grinder over the king's nail. 'Just a teensy bit more,' she told the boy.

'It isn't fair,' he whimpered.

'*Life* isn't fair,' the Dream Witch shrugged. 'And that, my pet, is the scariest nightmare of all.'

HAPPY ENDING?

'Let's hope we never see Leo again,' Milo said as he and Olivia made their way out of the garden. 'I'll keep an eye out in case he follows us.'

Olivia nodded quietly. Her mind was far away – on those mornings when the sun would peek through the cracks of her turret shutters and she'd wake to see Ephemia staring solemnly at her from the next pillow. Or the times when she was little, playing court with her dolls and the nutcracker, Count Ostroff; she was queen and Ephemia was her lady-in-waiting wearing a doll's apron as a robe. It was a magical time, and now –

'Are you all right?' Milo asked.

Olivia shook her head. 'Ephemia. She'll never . . . we'll never . . .' Her eyes swam; she took a deep breath. 'I'll be all right. Once this is over I can grieve.'

She looked over her shoulder one last time, to see the garden where she'd lost her oldest friend. 'Milo.'

He turned as well. 'What?'

The garden behind them was now of normal size; the tallest tulip would hardly touch their knees and the lilac bushes were trimmed the height of their waists.

'I recognise this garden,' Olivia said. 'The bushes, the flowers, they're all arranged as in my castle courtyard. Good heavens, do you see the ivy growing on the walls behind it. It's all the same except that Gardener would never have allowed those dandelions.'

'What dandelions?' Milo asked.

Indeed, the dandelions were gone, as were all

the weeds. Milo and Olivia looked in wonder at the immaculate beds of colour.

'So there you are,' a familiar voice called out behind them. 'You had us so worried.'

'Mother?'

'Who else?' the spell-queen laughed. She ran to the princess, held her tight, and wept tears of joy. 'Your father and I never thought we'd see you again. I still can't believe it, though it's been a whole day since you've been back. Milo, dear boy, once again, I thank you from the bottom of my heart. What you endured to bring our girl home safe to us – the village children, too – and to spare this kingdom the evil of the Dream Witch now and forever – it's beyond all gratitude.'

Olivia and Milo looked at each other in shock.

'Is this a dream?' Olivia asked.

'The most wonderful dream in the world,' the spell-queen beamed. 'Our dream come true.' She gave her another hug.

'What are you talking about? How did we get here? What's going on?'

The spell-queen's face filled with concern. She held Olivia by the shoulders. 'Wait. You still don't remember? Either of you.'

'No,' Olivia shook her head.

'Still?' Milo said.

'It must be the shock.' The spell-queen touched their foreheads. 'Why, your fevers haven't gone down, poor dears. You need to be back in your beds. I'll fetch the doctor. I was right to be worried when the servants said you'd left your bedrooms.'

Olivia felt dizzy. The spell-queen eased her to the ground. For the first time, Olivia realised she was wearing her silk nightgown and slippers. Milo found himself in a linen nightshirt and a velvet robe.

'What happened?' Olivia asked. 'Where are the duke, Leo, and the Pretonians?'

'Gone,' her spell-mother said. 'Yesterday, at dawn, the Dream Witch's forest burst into flames. The two of you ran from the fire, leading all the lost children to safety. The Dream Witch flew high on her cleaver, blazing like an inferno. Flames shot from her nose. She let loose a cry of rage and exploded, turning the sky to night.'

'Can it be?' Olivia asked, barely daring to believe.

'At once, the duke and his soldiers fled in terror back to Pretonia,' the spell-queen nodded. 'The two of you told such stories: about a dead girl turning into a monster under the marsh ice, about giant insects and flesh-eating moles, and about dear old Ephemia being a mouse all these years and then being snatched by the witch's owl.'

'Yes, it's all true, it all happened,' Olivia said. 'But after that—'

'After that you remembered nothing,' the spell-queen said. 'You couldn't say how you rescued the children, indeed had no memory of it happening. You said you felt like you'd wakened from a nightmare. Then the two of you passed out from exhaustion and terror, burning up with fever. You've slept a day and a night and here you are.'

'So it seems,' Milo said. He pinched himself. 'Then we're alive. We've left the dream world.'

'It feels so strange,' Olivia said. 'Like waking from a dream that felt real.'

'It *was* real, while you were in it,' the spell-queen said. 'But now you're safe and sound.'

Servants began to spill into the courtyard. 'They're here. All's well,' they called back to others inside.

'Olivia,' the spell-queen said, 'we've set up a bed for you in our room. We'll be right there if you ever cry out in your sleep. It's for our sake, too. We've had such dreams of you being lost to us forever. Being able to open our eyes and see you – I can't tell you how much that means.'

Olivia had a twinge of worry. 'But if I'm in your room, what about my pysanka, keeping it safe? Will we all be barred up as I was before?'

The spell-queen smoothed a hair from Olivia's forehead. 'No, my love. The Dream Witch is gone. The Great Dread is over. You can live like a normal child again.'

'And what about me? When can I see Mama and Papa?' Milo asked.

'As soon as you'd like. You collapsed before you could tell us where you lived.'

'In a burnt-out home at the foot of a hill between the marsh and the cornfield by the forest. You'll spot my father; he has a wooden foot.'

The spell-queen turned to a footman. 'Fetch them here in our finest coach.' She turned back to Milo. 'For your services to our girl and to our kingdom, your family will henceforth live at court.'

Milo leapt for joy. 'That was my dream when I took the witch's gold coins. Now here it is! It's happened!'

'Don't exert yourself,' the spell-queen warned. 'You still haven't properly recovered, and need your rest. We'll put you in Olivia's old turret room until your family's suite is ready. As you know, it has the best view of the countryside.'

Olivia and Milo looked to each other in happy confusion, as smiling servants wrapped

them in blankets, and put them on golden lit-
ters to be carried to their quarters.

'Mother, can this really be?' Olivia asked, eyes
welling with joy.

'It can,' the spell-queen said. She kissed her
forehead. 'Welcome home.'

THE SECRET IN THE ARMOIRE

So this is what it's like to be important, Milo thought, as he was carried up the staircase. It was certainly more fun than being dragged down to the dungeon by armed guards.

Once in the turret room, the servants tucked him into bed under fresh linen sheets, but he was too excited to stay there. As soon as they left, he raced to the window to breathe in the view of the countryside. To his delight, he saw his home beyond the hills.

But something was strange. He could still see the witch's forest; it looked unchanged. Hadn't Olivia's mother said it had suffered a great fire?

Milo wondered where the coach was, too, that was supposed to be going to pick up his parents. There was no sign of it below in the courtyard or on the cobblestoned road leading from the castle.

His thoughts were interrupted by a tickle of laughter, high and otherworldly. He turned around. There was no one there.

Little voices whispered his name in sing-song from inside the armoire: *Milo . . . Milo . . . Milo . . .*

Milo smiled. It must be the servant children hiding from him. Now that he'd be living in the castle they'd be new friends. He went to the armoire and threw open the doors. It was just as it was when he'd been transported here through the bats' wing parchment: a cupboard with dolls and toys hanging from its walls and sitting on its shelves. But where were the children?

Milo . . . Milo . . .

Was there a secret compartment somewhere at the back? There must be, Milo thought. He went inside and stepped forward. The door slammed shut behind him. Milo jumped with fright, then laughed at himself. His nerves were on edge after everything he'd been through, but, truly, what was there to be afraid of now? Surely a little breeze from the window had blown the door shut. He groped around for an inside handle. There wasn't one.

He knocked on the door. 'Hello? Can anyone hear me? Can someone let me out?'

There were titters all around him in the dark.

Milo didn't know whether to be scared or angry. 'What's so funny?'

'You.' The voice was that of a little girl, maybe five or six.

Milo relaxed. 'All right. Now that you and your friends have had your fun, please open the door?'

'We can't,' the little girl laughed.

Milo was annoyed. Still, he didn't want the servant children to think he was a cry-baby. 'I don't want to spoil your joke,' he said, 'but I've just gone through the worst time of my life. So, really, unlock the door. I'd like us to be friends.

I'm going to be living here, after all.'

'Oh you're going to be living here all right,' a strange voice clacked. 'You'll be here forever and ever.'

Milo froze. This wasn't the voice of a child. It was the voice of an old man. And what was that clacking sound when he spoke? 'Who are you? What do you want?'

'Guess,' said a woman, slyly.

More titters.

'At least let me see you.'

'As you wish.' A light went on. It came from a tiny lamp held by a tiny lady standing on the shelf by his head. Milo gasped; he'd seen her before. She was one of Olivia's dolls.

Milo looked around in panic. There were stuffed dolls circled all around him, with heads of brightly painted papier maché, birchwood, and china. Only the faces weren't as friendly as he'd remembered. Instead, they had a surly look, with sneaky smiles and shifty eyes.

'He looks surprised,' said a milkmaid with a cracked chin.

'Very surprised,' echoed an acrobat.

A commanding figure stepped out of the shadows. He was made of solid oak, with a military uniform decorated with gold leaf, and a chiselled face with pink cheeks, red lips, and black eyes. His jaw had been carved separately; it had a white beard and was hinged to a sturdy lever that ran out of his back.

Milo's eyes went wider yet. He suddenly understood the clacking sound he'd heard. It was Olivia's nutcracker. 'Count Ostroff!'

'Salute, peasant,' the nutcracker said. 'I rule this armoire.'

'But this is impossible,' Milo gasped, saluting. 'Toys can't talk.'

'In dreams we can,' the milkmaid said.

'But I'm awake.'

'Are you?'

'Yes. I went through the witch's dream world and woke up in the castle courtyard.'

Howls of nasty laughter.

'Correction,' Count Ostroff said darkly. 'You didn't wake up. You only *imagined* you woke up.

You're still in the witch's world.'

Milo was filled with a sickening horror. Of course, that would explain everything: Why he couldn't remember rescuing the village children. Why the witch's forest looked unharmed. But if he was still in the witch's world, then, even worse – the queen who greeted them in the courtyard wasn't Olivia's mother. She was a creature of the Dream Witch. He and the princess were in danger of their lives.

'What do you want with me?'

Two clown dolls leapt out of a knitting basket with a pair of long, sharp scissors. 'Fun,' they giggled. 'We want fun.' They each took a handle of the scissors: 'Snip, snip snip.'

Ladies-in-waiting dolls hoisted pins and needles. 'Sew, sew, sew.'

Milo recoiled. 'What do you mean?'

'We mean we're going to turn you into a doll for Olivia,' Count Ostroff explained.

'No!'

'Yes,' Count Ostroff said. 'First, we'll cut you open and take out your meat. Then we'll stuff you with straw and paint you bright as buttons.'

'Pretty dolly, pretty dolly,' the dolls sang happily.

Milo screamed and heaved himself at the four walls. They wouldn't budge.

'There's no escape,' the count clacked gleefully.

Two dolls began to crawl up Milo's legs. He tried to shake them off, but toppled to the ground. The acrobats had tied his feet with ribbons.

Dolls swarmed Milo's limbs, pinning him to the floor. A baby doll sat on his chest with a knitting needle in its chubby hands. 'Can I poke out his eyes?' it gurgled. 'Then he won't have to see what's happening.'

'Leave me alone!' Milo howled.

'And spoil the party?' the count clacked.

A voice rang out from the top of the armoire: 'If it's a party you want, it's a party I'll give you!'

The tiny lady raised her lamp. There was a mouse perched in a popped-out knothole at the top of the armoire.

'Ephemia?' Milo exclaimed. 'But you're dead!'

'Apparently not,' Ephemia squeaked. She threw back her head and let loose a cry of the wild. It soared up from the underworld into the burrows and tunnels beneath the forest floor, its pitch beyond human hearing. The glass on the tiny lady's lamp cracked.

Suddenly, there was a scurry in the walls around the armoire. Squirrels and chipmunks spilled in from every conceivable nook and cranny.

'To the rescue!' Ephemia cried in the language of the woods.

Ephemia's troops pounced on the demon dolls. With a grand chatter, china heads cracked on the ground, and claws tore papier maché. Meanwhile, little teeth chewed through knit body socks and snipped the stitching of cotton limbs.

'Eek!' the acrobats shrieked, as their legs fell off.

'Ack!' the clowns cried, as chipmunks stuffed

their cheeks with stuffing and ran off with their insides.

In no time, the dolls had vanished, taken to line the nests of the forest. Only Count Ostroff remained.

'What shall become of me?' he wailed as squirrels dragged him to a rat hole.

'For all your sins, you must spend the rest of your days cracking nuts for my friends,' Ephemia said. 'If not, you'll make a wonderful toy for them to gnaw on.'

The squirrels chittered their goodbyes.

'Thank you for saving my life!' Milo called after them, and then to Ephemia: 'And, above all, thanks to you. But how did you survive the owl? We saw you in its talons.'

'That was another wee mouse, alas. When I saw the owl, I ran for my life and hid for what seemed like forever.'

'Then how did you find me?'

Ephemia wriggled her nose. 'We beasties have a powerful sense of smell. In your case, a mixed blessing.'

'Uh, thanks,' Milo said. 'Did you find Olivia, too?'

Ephemia shook her head. 'I tried, but her scent's been masked.'

Milo frowned. 'The Dream Witch conjured a vision of Olivia's mother. It told her she didn't need her pysanka anymore. Then it led her to a dream of the royal bedroom.'

'Oh dear, we haven't got much time,' Ephemia fretted. 'But where to look? In dream-land, palace walls can shift as fast as thought.'

'I've got it,' Milo said. 'We don't *look*, we *smell*. Imagine the odours in a royal suite that might block Olivia's scent, Ephemia. Then follow your nose.'

THE SMELL OF WITCHCRAFT

Olivia was in her parents' bedroom, as conjured by the Dream Witch. She'd seen her spell-father propped up in his bed and hugged him close. He'd tapped his blessing on her cheek with his left thumb, then she'd gone with her spell-mother into the adjacent bathing room to soak away the grime of dreamland.

Her nose filled with a wondrous blend of aromas. Her mother's large porcelain tub, with its golden feet and faucets, had been filled with a bubble bath infused with orange blossoms and rose petals. Essential oils of jasmine, juniper, and eucalyptus hung in silver pans over lavender-scented candles.

The spell-queen sat on a stool at the head of the tub, combing Olivia's newly-washed hair with a brush dipped in freshly squeezed lemons.

'Your bedroom doesn't look like I remember it at all,' Olivia said.

'Doesn't it?' her spell-mother said. 'I suppose that's not surprising. You were locked up in your turret for so many years, you missed out on all the changes. I hope they don't disappoint you.'

'Oh, not at all,' Olivia reassured her. 'It's good to be home.' She looked down at the pysanka, dangling from the chain around her neck. It seemed to glow in an unfamiliar way.

The spell-queen eyed the talisman. 'I'll know you're truly well, my love, when you get rid of that thing.'

'Why? It's beautiful.'

The spell-queen shook her head. 'It's nasty. Such bad memories.'

Olivia frowned. 'All the same, I'm so used to having it near me, I'd feel odd if it were gone.'

'You mustn't be afraid of change,' the spell-queen soothed.

'I'm not, it's just – this was my christening gift from Ephemia. It wouldn't feel right to part with it.'

'But—'

Before her mother could say another word, Olivia decided to change the subject. 'How long have I been soaking? I feel like a prune.'

She rose from the tub and let her mother wrap her in a thick towel warmed over a bed of smouldering pine needles. Then she stepped behind the changing screen where ladies-in-waiting began to dress her in fresh petticoats and a sunny yellow gown with a cream bodice, pearl buttons, and lace trim.

'Ephemia was a good and faithful servant,' the spell-queen called over the screen. 'The pysanka was a token of her love, and I'm pleased you're loyal to her memory. But do you think she'd want you tethered to your past?'

'I can't hear you,' Olivia lied. 'Wait till I come out.'

'Surely Ephemia would want you to have a future as fresh as tomorrow,' the spell-queen continued a little more loudly. 'Come, let's get your father's advice.'

Olivia was cross that her mother kept pestering her. Still, she didn't want to be cranky – not on her second day home, and when her mother meant so well. 'Fine. As soon as I'm dressed.'

'But you *are* dressed,' the spell-queen said.

Olivia blinked. It was true: She *was* dressed. *How did that happen so quickly?* she wondered. *And when did I slip into these beaded shoes?*

Olivia looked up in confusion. To her further surprise, the ladies-in-waiting were gone and she was sitting between her mother and father on her parents' bed. The shock made her woozy.

'I'm not well,' she gasped. 'Time is playing the strangest tricks on me.'

The spell-queen eased her down onto the pillow. 'Rest. A little sleep will do you good.'

Olivia pressed her father's hand against her cheek and drifted off. She dreamed she was in the witch's world, lying on a rock bed between two demon serpents made of hair and finger-nails stuck together with bits of blood and skin.

Now, do it now, one said.

The other removed its hand from beneath her cheek and began to remove the pysanka hanging from her neck.

Olivia woke with a start. She found herself staring into her father's eyes. There was something strange in the blacks of his pupils: little shavings swimming in their gaze.

'Father?' She clutched for her pysanka and felt his hand around it. 'What are you doing?'

'N-nothing,' her spell-father stammered.

Olivia filled with terror. 'You're talking. You're moving. You're not my father! You're—'

'Give us the pysanka!' her spell-mother shrieked. 'Give it now or we'll rip out your throat.' Her hair shot out in all directions. Her teeth turned to fangs.

Olivia screamed.

'Not so fast, demon!' Milo cried. He shot out of the chimney beyond the bed, Ephemia on his shoulder.

'It takes more than jasmine and lemon to mask the scent of Hell!' Ephemia cried.

The spell creatures turned from Olivia. The skin fell from their forms. Their limbs disappeared into trunks of swelling sinew. They reared up from the ground like mighty snakes and undulated across the ceiling.

Milo pressed his back against the broad stone front of the fireplace. He tossed a coal scuttle on his head for a helmet and grabbed a poker and coal shovel from the hearth.

The snakes dropped on Milo, one after the other. He pierced one with the poker and bashed the other with the shovel. Instantly, they fell apart. The outer bits turned to dust, while the insides shattered into strands of hair and slivers of nail.

'Run!' Milo yelled.

Olivia didn't need to be told twice.

The pair ran into the corridor after Ephemia.

'To the left,' the good mouse cried.

Milo and Olivia turned left and ran past suits of armour. As they passed each suit it sprang to life and gave chase. Soon they were fleeing an army of ghostly warriors.

'Have a ride,' Milo hollered as they reached the main staircase. He leapt on the marble banister and slid down in a flash.

'Here goes nothing!' Olivia gulped, speeding after him.

The suits of armour weren't so nimble. The first few fell off the rail and crashed below. The others tried the stairs. They tripped and tumbled, clattering down in a twisted ball of chainmail and steel. They lurched to untangle themselves, clunking and clanking in pointless frenzy.

Meanwhile, Olivia and Milo raced through the palace gates with Ephemia. The dream castle disappeared in smoke, the gardens withered, and the friends found themselves running over rock. They were back in the witch's underworld, in a cavern as large as nightmare.

The rock floor sheered off in front of them, falling into a bottomless pit. They turned to run back, but the rock behind them had disappeared. They were on a ledge. It began to break into columns. Lava bubbled beneath. Sulphurous clouds billowed up from the cracks.

As the columns crumbled, Milo pointed across the chasm. 'Over there,' he hollered above the roar. 'It's the entrance to the witch's lair. It's where she flew me.'

'But how are we to reach it?' Olivia hollered back.

'We'll fly!' Ephemia cried. She opened her throat and roared to her woodland cousins roosting in the cavernous heights.

A great wind blew down from above. Olivia and Milo looked up to see thousands of bats swarming towards them. A second cry from Ephemia and the winged rodents swooped into rows of a hundred, fifty abreast, five deep.

'They look like flying carpets,' Olivia marvelled.

'Hop aboard,' Ephemia said. 'Lie flat to spread your weight.'

Milo let himself fall forward. He rolled over thousands of furry backs.

Olivia fell, too, Ephemia clinging to her ear. She missed her mark and plummeted towards the molten lava. Her carpet of bats dived after. They spread their wings and whooshed beneath her. Some rubbed their heads on Olivia's chin in welcome. Then her carpet flew up to join Milo's. They headed towards the witch's lair.

'Wait for me!' called a voice from the mists.

'Leo?'

'I followed you. Spare me,' he wailed.

Olivia and Milo gritted their teeth.

'There's things you do because you have to,' Ephemia said.

'I know, I know,' Olivia replied. She said a prayer, as the flying rodents circled back to rescue the puling brat. The bats at the edges of each formation peeled away to form a third flying carpet.

'I'm so grateful,' Leo wept, once safely aboard.

'See that you stay that way,' Ephemia sniffed. 'These bats can fly upside down.'

There was no more time to talk. They'd crossed the gulf and entered the Dream Witch's lair.

IN THE DREAM
WITCH'S LAIR

The bats flew down a pitch-black corridor.
They veered left and right, soared high and low.

Olivia and Milo kept their eyes closed. It was
far more comforting to pretend the passage was
well lit, than to witness a flight into nothingness.

Ephemia felt Olivia's tension. 'Never fear,'
she encouraged, 'our friends see in the dark; the
night is their home.'

Nice words. But with the air whistling in her
ears and her hair flying out behind her, Olivia
was far from reassured. Her only comfort was

that Leo was throwing up *behind* them; if he'd been in the lead . . .

'Ah, the antechamber to the witch's quarters,' Ephemia announced.

Olivia opened her eyes. She wished she hadn't. The chamber was carved from the rock in the shape of a mouth. Its walls were lit by flaming skull-pots set into alcoves that glistened like oozing flesh. At the end of the chamber was an iron door crusted with rust and lichens. The latch was shaped like a devil's head with an open jaw.

'Can that really be the entrance?' Milo asked.

'Yes,' Ephemia said, as the bats spiralled to the ground.

'Strange. From the other side it looked enormous.'

'It wasn't; you were small. The Dream Witch shrunk you to fit into her spice grinder.'

The bats deposited their riders and flew to the top of the antechamber, where they hung by their feet from gnarly outcrops of rock. Leo held back as the friends approached the door.

'How do we get in?' Olivia asked.

'Try the latch,' Ephemia replied.

'It's as easy as that?'

'The Dream Witch doesn't get visitors. Why would she keep it locked?'

Olivia reached for the devil's-head latch, taking care to keep her fingers underneath its chin. The moment she squeezed, the jaw snapped shut, the latch opened, and the iron door swung wide on its rusty hinges. Olivia heard the sound of bottles rattling on the wooden shelves within.

'It's all right,' Milo called out to the children. 'It's me, the boy the Dream Witch sent to the castle. I've come with friends to set you free. And not just any friends: the Princess Olivia, her court mentor, and a Pretonian prince.'

'This is a trick,' said a little voice.

'And a mean one,' said another. 'Princess Olivia is the reason we're here. She doesn't care about us.'

'I care a great deal,' Olivia said, feeling her way through the dim light. 'It's wrong that you've suffered for my safety. That's why I'm here – to make things right.'

The bottles stopped rattling as the children pressed their faces against their jars to get a better look.

'Is it her?' one whispered.

'Can't tell,' another whispered back. 'I've only seen her once, up in that turret behind the bars.'

'Have a closer look,' Olivia said. She took the child's spice grinder off the shelf and held it to her face. Inside, she saw a terrified boy in rags. 'Don't be afraid. I make you all a promise. In no time, my friends and I will have you home again, safe in your parents' arms.'

'The Dream Witch will kill you first,' the boy said. 'She wants your heart.'

'She can want it all she likes,' Olivia replied, with far more confidence than she felt. 'But it's mine, I'm keeping it, and that's that.'

Foul gusts of wind blew in from the antechamber.

'It's her,' Ephemia said. 'She's coming back. Hide.'

'Where?' Olivia panicked.

'Here!' Milo pointed to the coal staircase leading down to the witch's spell chamber. Leo bolted down the steps.

Olivia returned the spice grinder to its shelf. 'We mustn't raise her suspicions. Everything must look the way it was,' she whispered. 'But we'll be back to get you out as soon as we can.' She and Milo disappeared down the stairs, Ephemia scampering at their heels.

No sooner were they out of sight than the Dream Witch flew in on her cleaver, the great owl on her shoulder. She hopped off at the grinder shelves. 'What's going on? Who opened the door?'

The jars rattled. 'It wasn't us.'

'Then who was it?' the Dream Witch demanded.

The cleaver reared up, as if to slice a row of the bottles from their shelves. The children shrieked.

'No wait. Don't tell me.' The Dream Witch unwrapped her trunk from around her waist and sniffed the air. 'Jasmine, and lemon, with a hint of mole pantry.' She followed her nose to the top of the stairs. 'Aren't we the brave souls?'

The sorceress spun to the outer entrance of her lair. '*Finitum transitorum nexit!*' She snapped her bony fingers: the iron door clanged shut. Its edges turned molten red and melded with the rock.

'A perfect seal,' the Dream Witch cackled. She turned to the coal stairs leading down to her study. 'They'll never escape me now.'

BETRAYAL

Olivia, Milo, and Ephemia dashed into the witch's spell chamber.

Leo was already there, running in circles. Each time he neared one of the nightmarish murals, the creatures in the picture reared up as if to leap off the canvas. Then Leo screamed and ran headlong towards another and another and another: 'Where-do-we-hide, where-do-we-hide, where-do-we-hide?'

Milo glanced in all directions. When he'd been shrunk to fit in a spice grinder, he could have disappeared behind a bundle of chicken's feet, a basket of herbs, or up a hobnailed boot. Not now. 'The shadows.' He pointed to the end of the cavern.

'Yes,' Olivia echoed. 'Find a crack in the rock wall.'

They fled past the witch's writing table and spell books, towards her monstrous portrait.

'It's alive!' Olivia gasped.

'Yes,' Milo said grimly. 'It's made of snakes, beetles, and toads all pinned to an oak board.'

Ephemia sent the creatures a thought – *We'll rescue you, too, little ones.*

Milo spotted a rock crevasse to the right. 'In here.'

Leo elbowed past him. Olivia and Milo squeezed in after. No sooner were they out of sight than the Dream Witch sailed into the room on her cleaver.

'Come out, come out, wherever you are,' the sorceress sang, as her owl swooped around the ceiling. 'You can't hide. I don't even have to use my nose. Your thumping hearts give you away.'

Leo gulped. 'There's no reason all of us

should get caught,' he whispered, and shoved Milo and Olivia out of the crevasse with his boot.

'What have we here?' the Dream Witch cooed. 'A princess, a peasant, and a mouse.'

The owl flew at Ephemia with a screech; the little mouse leapt to safety in a cranny between the spell books.

'Don't worry, Doomsday, you'll catch her yet,' the witch cackled.

'Shame on the both of you,' Olivia exclaimed. 'You're nothing but bullies, preying on innocent children and woodland creatures.'

'Hoo hoo,' the owl laughed coldly, and settled on the Dream Witch's shoulder.

The sorceress scratched its ear. 'Hoo hoo, indeed. Who-who are you to lecture me, Princess? Who-who to escape me, peasant? And who-who to continue to hide, my little Pretonian rascal? Yes, I mean you, Prince Leo. Show yourself.'

Leo slid from the crawl space, sweat dripping from his fingertips.

'Your heart's pounding more than all the others combined,' the Dream Witch mocked. She glided towards Olivia.

Olivia clutched her pysanka and held it before her. 'Stay back.'

The witch stepped back. 'Never mind, I can wait. The door to my lair has been sealed into the rock. Your only other escape is to leap into my murals, and be torn apart by the visions within.'

Inside the dreamscapes, the mantis clacked its mandibles, the mole scurried in its pantry, and the marsh monsters slapped their tentacles, as if eyeing lunch through a glass window.

'Sooner or later you'll all grow hungry,' the Dream Witch continued. 'Then what? Which of your friends will betray you for a chance to escape?'

'I will!' Leo exclaimed. He grabbed the pysanka from Olivia's outstretched hand and ran towards the sorceress.

'Stop!' Olivia cried.

She and Milo tried to catch him, but the

Dream Witch tossed them back with the wave of a hand.

'That was fast,' the witch said to Leo. 'I thought you'd at least wait for a tummy rumble.'

'Why?' Leo asked, stopping ten feet short. 'You made me a deal in the woods. You said if I destroyed the pysanka, you'd give me more treasure than my father has ever seen.'

'Traitor,' Olivia shouted.

'Sticks and stones,' Leo sneered back.

'Very well, then,' the Dream Witch smiled. 'Destroy it.'

'Not so fast,' Leo said. 'I'm not stupid. As long as I have the pysanka, you can't hurt me. But once I destroy it, who says you'll keep your promise?'

The Dream Witch splayed her fingernails across her chest. 'You don't trust me?'

'Take me to your treasury so I can see my prize,' Leo continued nervously. 'Once I have it safely in Pretonia, I'll smash the talisman into a million pieces.'

'You're quite the negotiator, aren't you?' the Dream Witch said.

Leo puffed out his chest. 'Oh yes. I'm brilliant, despite what Father thinks. But I'll show him. With my new wealth, he'll love me and I can do as I please. First thing, I'll make Uncle clean our stables.'

'Come then, let's see your reward,' the Dream Witch said. 'Just spare me a moment to take your friends' hearts.'

'No,' Leo panicked. 'I don't want to see. I don't want to hear. I don't want to know.'

'A coward to the end,' the Dream Witch said darkly, 'afraid to look at the cost of their treasure?'

Leo flushed. 'Take me away. Now.'

The Dream Witch tossed back her head. '*Vamamos vamimus treasuratus.*' She snapped her fingers. Instantly, Leo was floated up the stairs, magically transported through the solid iron door, and whisked to her treasury.

The Dream Witch tucked her nose around her waist. 'I won't be long,' she said to the friends. 'If you get bored, think on the horrors to come.' With that, she hopped on her cleaver and vanished.

Milo gritted his teeth. 'What do we do now?'

'I have a plan,' Olivia said. 'Follow me.' She ran up the staircase, Milo at her heels.

Ephemia stayed behind. She sniffed around the spell books. 'You were mine, once. Remember? Oh, what has the Dream Witch done to you? What has she made you do?'

Odours of old potions clung to the parchments. Ephemia's whiskers twitched.

Memories stirred.

TREASURE FOREVER

Leo found himself on a solid gold platform high above the ground. Below, a field of treasure extended in all directions as far as he could see. Mountains of golden goblets spilled onto banks of marble urns overflowing with rubies and diamonds. Jade sculptures of peacocks faced armies of bronze stallions. Fountains of agate, amber and lapus lazuli shot jets of emeralds and pearls into the air. And every inch between was thick with gold coins.

Leo shielded his eyes from the glare of the glitter. 'Mine. All mine,' he exulted.

'You're pleased?' asked the Dream Witch, hovering on her cleaver.

'It's more than I ever dreamed of,' Leo confessed. 'Now, all that's left is for you to bring it to my father's court.'

'Your father's court?' The Dream Witch scratched her head with her nose. 'I'm afraid that's not part of our bargain.'

'Suit yourself,' Leo said smugly. 'But if you don't, I won't break the pysanka.'

'Fine by me,' the witch replied. 'Now that it's no longer near the princess, why should I care?'

Leo blinked. 'Because . . . because . . .' he stomped his foot. 'Look, if you *don't* help me, how am I to get my treasure home?'

'Who said anything about going home?' the witch said innocently.

Leo's heart beat a little faster. 'What do you mean?'

'I mean no more than I say,' the sorceress smiled.

She waved her hand. All around, gold coins rose up from the ground. They clinked and jangled in the air, swirling around the platform like leaves in a windstorm. They began to whirl higher. Before he knew it, Leo found himself in the eye of a golden tornado.

A coin nicked his ear. A dozen clipped his legs. Leo dropped to his knees and shielded his head with his hands. 'Stop! Make them stop!'

'As you wish.'

The Dream Witch waved her hand again and the coins fell from the sky in columns. They circled the golden platform and melded into the bars of a cage. Silver plates spun up into a roof. A diamond rope and a brass bar attached themselves as a swing.

Leo struggled to squeeze between the golden bars, but they were too tight. His body began to itch and prickle. Spines sprouted from his flesh. Yellow feathers burst from his face and neck, and out of the elbows and ankles of his armour. His fingers disappeared. His toes turned into claws. He hopped around his cage in terror.

Let me out. Let me out, Leo screamed. But all

that escaped his beak was a frantic chirp.

'Yes, sing to me, my little canary,' the Dream Witch cackled. 'Sing to me in your gilded cage. You dreamed of treasure forever, and you shall have it.'

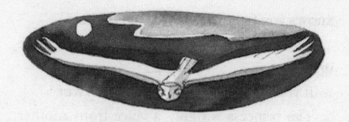

THE FINAL
NIGHTMARE

Olivia and Milo ran up the staircase into the grinder room.

'We're back, like we promised,' Olivia called out.

They each took a bottle off a shelf and went to unscrew the lids.

'What are you doing?' cried the girl in Olivia's jar.

'Taking you to your parents.' Olivia grunted.

'No. Put me back. The Dream Witch will be angry.'

'Don't worry. You'll be home before she even

knows you're gone.'

'I won't, I won't. She'll catch us and grind me up.'

'If you stay, she'll grind you up anyway.'

'The princess is right,' a voice from another jar chimed in. 'Last week I lost my toes. Next time, maybe my legs.'

The other jars agreed: 'It's our only chance,' one said. 'Take us too,' said some others. 'Hurry,' from all.

But speed was impossible. The lids of the grinders were screwed tight.

'There's too many bottles to hold in our arms,' Olivia whispered to Milo, 'but the Dream Witch will destroy everyone we leave behind. What do we do?'

Milo pointed to two large wicker baskets in the corner, one filled with chicken's feet, the other with entrails. 'We can carry them in those.'

They tossed the offal aside and filled the hampers with the jars. Just as they were done, the Dream Witch's merry song echoed up the tunnel beyond the antechamber.

For my spells a special must
Boys and girls all ground to dust.
But for perfection of my art
I need a little princess heart.

Milo grabbed a hamper. 'Run.'

Olivia tucked the last jar under her neck, grabbed the second hamper and raced Milo down the coal stairs. The baskets swung wildly. The children squealed.

'Sorry,' Milo said. 'Close your eyes. Pretend you're on a swing.' He and Olivia burst back into the study.

'Ephemia,' Olivia exclaimed, 'what have you discovered?'

'Not much,' Ephemia replied. 'I can smell a shape-changing spell in that red book over there, but it's too scared to open at the incantation. In fact, the entire library is scared. The witch has cracked some of their spines, ripped their pages . . .'

The leather covers trembled.

'Never mind,' Olivia said to the books.

'Perhaps you can help us when we defeat the witch.'

'If,' Milo said.

'*When*,' Olivia declared.

A shriek from the top of the stairs shook the cavern. Chunks of coal fell from the ceiling.

'She's here. We're going to die!' cried the bottles.

'No, we're not,' Olivia said. She ran to the witch's writing desk. 'Milo, do you remember the spell-words the Dream Witch used to transport you to my armoire?'

'How could I forget? *Transitorus vitissimo*. It's what she said to send me and what she taught me to say to bring you back.'

'Perfect,' Olivia said. She grabbed the owl's quill, dipped it in the witch's inkwell and began to scribble a picture of her parents' bedroom on one of the bat-wing parchments.

'WHERE HAVE YOU TAKEN MY SPELL-FOOD?' the Dream Witch raged above.

'Milo, hide the baskets. Ephemia, prepare an ambush,' Olivia said, drawing furiously.

Ephemia dived into a mound of herbs, as Milo tossed a dirty sheet over the hampers.

'Sniff them out, nose,' the Dream Witch commanded. The sound of her hobnailed boots echoed down the coal stairs.

'Olivia, hide,' Ephemia pleaded.

'I can't! I haven't finished drawing yet!'

'Please.'

Too late. The witch's nose snaked in from the stairwell. The Dream Witch followed, Doomsday on her shoulder.

Olivia set down her quill and rose to greet her foe.

'So there you are, Princess,' the Dream Witch crowed. 'I've been waiting for this moment ever since your christening. You were stupid to enter my world.'

'How could I stay safe in my castle and let you grind the kingdom's children?'

'Conscience has a cost,' the witch sneered.

'What do you know about conscience?'

'Enough to know it's lost you your life and destroyed your parents. So tell me, how shall their promise be fulfilled? Do I pluck out your heart with my fingernails? Or should my nose tear down your throat and rip it from your chest?'

The nose coiled, ready to strike.

'I think your trunk should tear itself apart,' Olivia said. 'Ephemia, now!'

Ephemia leapt from the mound of herbs to the writing desk. In a single bound, she sprang into a flying double-somersault, landing on the witch's nose. She gave it a bite.

The Dream Witch howled and swatted her face, as Ephemia scurried into her left nostril and up the trunk, tickling with every paw pad. The witch went wild. There was no way to itch. She slapped her nose against the cavern walls, whapping up a storm of coal dust. The nose let loose a mighty sneeze but Ephemia held fast to its forest of hairs, and kicked and scratched with her claws.

Doomsday came to the witch's aid. He dived at Olivia. Milo threw a skull at his head. It clipped the owl's left shoulder. The bird screeched away, nursing its wounded wing.

In all the confusion, Olivia seized her chance. She grabbed the inkwell and splashed its ooze across the witch's face. The muck sizzled and steamed on the Dream Witch's eyes: Her vision blurred; her red coals blackened.

'Olivia, the witch's portrait, look!' Milo cried. 'What's happening to her is happening to it!'

Olivia glanced at the far wall. The mosaic wriggled in frenzy. Shells of red paint fell off the toads that were pinned for the picture's eyes.

'The witch – she must have made the portrait in order to bind nature to her will,' Olivia exclaimed.

'Of course,' Milo said. 'For stronger spells!'

'Quick, set the creatures free,' Ephemia hollered down a nostril.

Olivia and Milo raced to the mosaic as the Dream Witch staggered to her feet. The sorceress reared her great proboscis. 'You'll pay!' She staggered towards them. '*Praditar—*'

But before she could cast her spell, Ephemia bit inside the base of her nose. '*Prandi—*

TAAA— AAA!!!' The nose flailed.

Olivia removed the pin of a beetle stuck to the portrait's lip. As it buzzed into the air, a wart popped off the witch's mouth. Milo freed four snakes on the picture's nose. Ropes of skin slithered from the witch's trunk.

The sorceress lurched forward, eyes steaming, flesh peeling. Her long yellow fingernails slashed the air. Milo and Olivia unpinned a dozen locusts, and the fingernails snapped off. Two steps more and the Dream Witch collapsed, falling apart as newts and salamanders, frogs and lizards, hopped and scurried their way to freedom.

Ephemia leapt out of the witch's eye socket and onto Olivia's shoulder. 'Look,' she squeaked.

As the Dream Witch broke apart, the dreamscapes on her walls were breaking up too: the mole pantry vanished in a billow of bilious gas. The marsh monsters exploded with the last trumpet of her nose. Everywhere, visions of hell were torn to pieces as surely as the demon who created them.

The last of the Dream Witch twitched at Olivia's feet. She was now no more than a pair of lips. 'I took only what the world gave me,' the lips screeched. 'Its hopes and fears.'

'Yes, and made us live in nightmare,' Olivia snapped.

She loosened the last of the great mosaic – six large grey moths. They fluttered away in silence and the Dream Witch was no more.

All around, the spell books clapped their covers in applause. But it was too early for celebration. An ominous rumble roiled up from the belly of the earth. The walls of the cavern began to crack and splinter.

'No time to lose,' Olivia exclaimed, 'As the witch went, so goes her underworld.'

She and Milo raced for the children in the hampers, as the cavern split apart. 'I've drawn my parents' bedroom on this bat-wing parchment,' she said to Milo. 'Repeat the words the Dream Witch used to transport you.'

'*Transitorrus vittissimo!*' Milo roared.

The parchment on the writing table spread

its wings. It stretched across the floor.

'Here we go,' Olivia said.

She grabbed a hamper and ran onto the magic drawing, Ephemia snuggled by her ear. Milo grabbed the other basket and followed her. The spell books followed too. They flapped their covers and flew about the picture, hovering safely around the princess and her friends.

The sides of the parchment rose high above them. The edges enveloped them. As the cavern walls exploded all around, the parchment vanished into thin air.

DAWN

An hour before, in the world above, glimmers of dawn crept across the countryside, lighting the tips of the cornstalks, the reeds along the marsh banks, and the stream of families making their way to the castle. All night rumours had spread from village to farmhouse. Peasants living near the marsh said they'd seen Prince Leo and his cavalry pursuing Princess Olivia towards the witch's forest.

Neighbours roused Milo's parents with the news. 'Word is, she escaped the castle with a friend to fight the Dream Witch.'

Milo's mother put her hand to her mouth. 'The children left last night, that must have been then. They were here. We helped them.'

'To think we've blamed the princess for our pain,' his father said. 'Yet she's risked her life for our children.'

'Lost her life, you mean,' the neighbour said.

Milo's father gripped his pitchfork. 'Let's go to the castle. They'll have news first. When it breaks, we can rejoice or grieve together.'

By the time they arrived, the square below the royal suite was filling rapidly. A wall of Pretonian soldiers stood between the crowd and the castle gates. Some citizens knelt in prayer. Others stood silently, staring up at the king and queen's balcony.

Milo's parents made their way to the front. There was a fanfare of trumpets. Leo's uncle swaggered out from the castle: 'Hear me, people of Bellumen,' he said, standing before them. 'As of last night, your king and queen are under my protection. I rule you now.'

There was a stunned silence. Then a voice

rang out from the crowd: 'Says who? Let the queen speak.' And another: 'Yes. Let's hear that from the queen.'

The duke bristled. His men grabbed their swords by the hilt. 'Clear the square,' he ordered.

Murmurs rippled through the congregation. A few peasants backed away, but Milo's parents thought only of their son. 'We'll never leave, sir,' his father said. 'Not till we hear about our children. From the queen.'

The duke struck him hard on the shoulder. 'Clear the square, I said. Go back to your homes.'

Milo's father wobbled on his wooden foot, but held his ground. 'Our homes are *here*,' he said bravely. 'Go home to *your* home.'

The crowd roared its approval.

The duke's neck bulged against his collar. 'You mock me?'

'No,' Milo's mother exclaimed. 'Striking the lame – you mock yourself.'

'Seize them!' the duke bellowed.

But before the soldiers could act, the crowd surged forward and surrounded Milo's parents. A voice cried out from the multitude. 'Seize all of us, why don't you?'

The duke peered warily at the rabble. Dawnlight glinted off thousands of farmers' rakes and pitchforks, spades and hoes. An armed rioting mob was the last thing he wanted without cannons in position. The duke whirled on his heel, re-entered the castle, and stormed up to the royal suite.

Olivia's mother had been at her husband's bedside changing the dressing where his nail had been severed. The sound of the people had stirred her to her feet as the duke barged in. 'How dare you burst in here after what you did to us last night?'

The duke ignored her. 'Speak to your people, Queen. Tell them we rule here now. Demand they return to their farms.'

'But they've come to hear about their children.'

'Their children are with the witch.'

'Olivia's gone to save them.'

'Your daughter's dead. The hair I plucked from your head and the nail I ripped from your husband was the price of my nephew. Your daughter's life was the trade.'

'Monster!' Queen Sophia flew at him.

The duke gripped her arms by the elbow. She tried to kick but he tossed her to the floor. 'Mark well: If your people refuse our commands, we'll mount the castle's cannons and blow them apart, every last man, woman, and child.'

'You wouldn't dare.'

'There's nothing I wouldn't dare.' The duke went to the king's bedside, grabbed a pillow in both hands and held it above the king's face. 'The Royal Vegetable can't move. He's this pillow and thirty seconds from heaven. Do I have your attention?'

'No! Stop!' the queen cried. Slowly, she rose from the ground, went to the balcony, and opened the doors.

At the sight of their ruler, the people cheered. 'Long live King Augustine. Long live Queen

Sophia. Long live Princess Olivia.'

The queen bowed to them and raised her hand. The people fell silent. She steadied herself on the balustrade. 'I know you long for news of your children. I have none. Forgive me. Forgive me, too, for my failure. For last night, the kingdom fell into barbarian hands. From this day forth you will be ruled by—'

Before she could continue, an explosion rocked the witch's forest. A mountain of earth and stone heaved high as the sky. From out of the hole came the howls of demons exposed to the light. Hordes of smoke-shapes flew into the air – the Dream Witch's monsters, ghouls, and other creatures of nightmare. The people fell to the ground and covered their heads as the visions burned in the sun. The smoke blackened the sky. Then a mighty whirlwind blew them apart, and all was fresh as spring.

At the same time, a giant parchment of bat wings appeared inside the royal suite. It hovered above the bed and unfurled itself. Olivia, Milo and Ephemia were at its centre with their baskets of bottles. The spell books flew around them.

'Mother! Father! We're home!' Olivia called out.

Jaws dropped. The guards fell back.

The parchment disintegrated. Olivia, Milo and the baskets bounced onto the mattress beside the king.

Olivia kissed her father's cheek. 'Father.' She ran towards the queen. 'Mother.'

The duke snapped his fingers. Guards stepped between Olivia and her mother. 'Save the greetings, Princess. Where's my nephew?'

'He took off with the Dream Witch, the traitor,' Olivia said smartly. 'I haven't seen him since and I hope I never will.'

'Say what you like, but do as I say. The kingdom has gathered outside the castle. Send them home. Tell them their children are dead.'

'But they aren't!' Milo exclaimed. 'They're here in these baskets.'

The duke blinked. 'In those jars?'

'Yes.'

But not for long. Back in the real world, the children returned to their proper size. The grinders popped like bottles of champagne, the splinters of witch-glass turning to air, as boys and girls burst free, laughing and squealing.

The guards froze in wonder. Olivia dived between their legs and joined her mother on the balcony. 'It's me, Olivia!' she shouted to the people below. 'The Dream Witch is vanquished. Your children are alive. They're here! Come, see for yourselves!'

A deafening cheer shook the square. Parents and grandparents, aunts and uncles, cousins and friends ran towards the castle gates.

'Order,' the soldiers hollered.

'Kill them,' the duke thundered.

There were too many. Soldiers raised their swords but were knocked to the ground and trampled underfoot. The line breeched, the rabble stormed through the gates and into the castle courtyard.

Faced with the roaring mob, the Pretonians fled for safety. Some stripped off their armour and deserted. Others hid in goat carts or jumped down wells. Still others hopped on the nearest horse and galloped away as fast as they could. Even the guards in the royal suite took flight as children continued to erupt from the grinders.

'Surrender, Duke,' Olivia ordered. 'Kneel before my mother and father and beg forgiveness.'

'Never!'

Ephemia jumped on top of the royal footboard and crossed her paws. 'In the words of the Bully of Pretonia: Say what you like, but do as she says.' She winked at Olivia.

In that second, the duke snatched Ephemia in his fist. 'You dare order my surrender, Princess? It is you who must kneel! Kneel now or I'll dash your friend's brains on the cobblestones below.'

He backed onto the balcony. High above, an owl with a wounded wing took note of the confusion – and of the little mouse in the outstretched hand.

The red spell book flew to Olivia's side. The

most abused of the witch's library, it suspended itself before the princess, and fluttered its torn pages. Olivia read the first thing she saw: '*Amnibia Pentius Prixus Pendor!*'

There was a puff of smoke. The duke found himself hoisting an ample old woman with bright blue eyes and two dozen whiskers. The next thing he knew, he was squashed under her bottom.

Ephemia got up. 'A rat!' she declared, pointing beneath her at the rodent crawling out of the duke's empty armour.

The rat turned in a circle. 'A rat? Where?'

'Why, if it isn't the Duke of Fettwurst,' Olivia laughed. 'Would you like some cheese?'

The rat looked in horror at the giants all around him. 'How did all of you get so big?' He shrieked at the sight of his paws. 'What are these?'

'Cage him,' Ephemia said.

'You'll never trap the Duke of Fettwurst,' the rat exclaimed. He scurried for a hole in the castle walls. Alas, he didn't get far. The great owl, diving for a mouse, had found a fatter feast. It snatched the rat in its talons.

'How dare you!' the rat huffed. 'Don't you know who I am? I'm the Duke of Fettwurst!'

'Hoo? Hoo?' Doomsday hooted and flew him away.

The children crowded around Olivia and Milo.

'Thank you,' said the girl who'd been so afraid. 'Without you, we wouldn't be alive.'

'You're welcome,' Olivia smiled. 'But you've more important people to see here than us. Quick, go, help each other to your families.'

'I want to see mine too,' Milo said quietly. 'If they'll remember me.'

'Of course they will,' Olivia said. 'With the Dream Witch gone, so is her curse. But Milo, when you've found them, please don't leave. We want your family to stay with us at the castle.'

Milo gave her a shy smile. Then, thinking he should do something, but not knowing what, he gave her a hug – 'Thanks. I'll see you later' –

and ran to find his parents.

He squeezed his way down the stairs, through a sea of reunions. His parents had struggled up to the staircase landing. He threw his arms around them.

'Mama, Papa, I'm sorry for all the grief I've caused,' he whispered, burying his head in their shoulders.

'No son,' his father said. 'Be proud of what you've done. We loved the boy in you. And now we love the man.'

Back in the royal suite, Queen Sophia held her daughter tight. 'You're home. You're home.'

They knelt beside the king's bedside. Olivia put his hand to her cheek. It was pale and cold. Still, he tapped gently with his thumb, as if to say, *My darling girl*, and gazed at her in adoration.

'I was so scared,' Olivia said, 'but I thought of you and prayed I wouldn't let you down. Oh, Mother, Father, I promise you, I never will. My fear will never overcome my love. Not ever.'

Her tears fell on her father's hand . . . and something strange began to happen. His fingers trembled.

Olivia and her mother looked at the king in wonder. 'Father?'

'Augustine?'

Olivia's father opened and closed his lips. They opened and closed again. Sounds began to struggle from his mouth, like water from a dry riverbed. 'O . . . O . . . li . . .'

'Father?'

'O . . . li . . . vi . . . a . . . Olivia.' Her father smiled. It was all that he could say for now. But it was enough.

Ephemia put her hand on Olivia's shoulder. 'The horrors that felled your father have vanished like the witch's curse. I tended his father and his grandfather before him. With your help and these magic books, we'll restore him good as new.'

'Indeed, we will,' her mother said.

Olivia was filled with the greatest joy she'd ever known. Home had never felt so good.

Here, free in her parents' love, the last of the Great Dread left her heart. In its place was hope for tomorrow.

A happy dream to last a lifetime and beyond.